The Robe of Love

The Robe of Love

Secret Instructions for the Heart

by Laura Simms

Codhill Press

NEW PALTZ NEW YORK

Library of Congress Cataloging-in-Publication Data

Simms, Laura.
    The robe of love: secret instructions for the heart / Laura Simms.
        p.cm.
    ISBN 1-930337-05-1 (alk. paper)
    1. Tales — Adaptions. I. Title.

    PS3569.I4789 R63 2002
    813'.54 — dc21

                                                    2002067501

Dedicated to my son Ishmael

The moment I heard my first story

I started looking for you.

—*Rumi*

Table of Contents

Acknowledgements

Without the confidence and friendship of David Appelbaum, who has always encouraged my writing, this book would not have happened. However, stretching back in time there are many whose generosity has urged *Robe*'s arrival: Terry Tempest Williams gently opened my animal eyes and ears. She taught me to birdwatch in wilderness and skyscrapers and have no fear of love. I am grateful to Joan Sutton for listening along the way and helping me to trust my voice. Thank you. Special thanks to Muriel Bloch and Gioia Timpanelli, whose storytelling touches my heart. They are each fearless lovers of love. To Pomme Clayton and Miranda Shaw for abundant conversations about story. Joseph Feinstein for also adoring the story of the Moon Cuckoo. To Frances Harwood, Naomi Newman, Gary Hoffman, Steve Gorn, Barbara Borden, Janice Rous, Bob Speers, Mary Platt, Merinell Phillips, Walter Feldman, Andrew Grieg, Liz Weir, and Shelley Pierce, who each taught me about love and friendship regardless of distances. I want to thank Amy Kolker for delightful hours of work and passionate conversations.

Acknowledgements

Years ago I had the good fortune to learn from Joseph Campbell, May Kedney, and Margaret Meade. Special thanks to Marlene Pitkow, Anita Graham, Angela Lloyd, and Amichai Lau Levi for stories. To Barbara Koltur, for mythic sport and faith in romance.

I could not have begun this book without the emotional support I received from Ariel Jordan, and Valerie Sanford. Vi Taqseblu Hilbert nurtured my ability to see beneath the surface of stories and bring them to life. Sharon Ascher who was there in the beginning. And, to my parents and my brother Norman. No one in my life taught me more about how to pry open the heart and awaken compassion and awareness than my teacher the Vidhyadara Chogyam Trungpa, Rinpoche. Also, Pema Chodron, Khenpa Pema Choepel, Lama Shedrup and His Holiness Tai Situ Rinpoche appeared on the path to wake me up when I fell asleep. And, I am ceaselessly grateful to Dzigar Kongtrul Rinpoche and his wife Elizabeth for teaching me to make friends with death and thus inspired a bigger view of love than I could have imagined.

To Ishmael Beah, Mohamad Beah, and Alusine Bah I have a special thanks. Being part of their stories taught me the truth that love can never be extinguished by war, by trauma or sorrow. And from them I received the secret love of mother trust. ❧

Foreword

Laura Simms is a storyteller. She belongs to the sacred tradition of the griot, the zyrau, the keeper of the talking stick. If you have had the privilege of hearing Laura tell a story in person, live, then you know what it means to be transported to another world and transformed in the process of listening.

I first heard Laura telling stories at the American Museum of Natural History in the spring of 1983. She was telling star stories. Her voice transcended thought. It was not what we heard, exactly, but more what we felt. The stories entered our bodies, became images that swam through our bloodstream, penetrated each cell, until we remembered who we are, where we came from, and all that binds us together as human beings. With each tale another wall in the museum came down, then the ceiling, until we were sitting outside looking up at the night sky with the Milky Way arching over us.

That night, Laura Simms changed my life.

I introduced myself as a young intern at the Museum of Natural History from Utah, living in New York City for three months. I explained to her that I was working with

Navajo children in the Four Corners region of the American Southwest on a storytelling project. The children were bringing what they knew through their traditional stories to their understanding of natural history in the desert. I told her the question that was burning in my heart was this: What stories do we tell that evoke a sense of place?

I will never forget how she listened, how her eyes met mine, and how she took this question seriously from a stranger and invited me to tea at her loft to discuss these matters in the privacy of her home. The conversation between us has never stopped. We have been holding these questions together ever since in our friendship of almost twenty years, telling each other stories that make us laugh and weep, at once.

It is in these tales of awe and wonder, struggle and courage, mystery and magic that we tell each other every day of our lives. They keep us sane and humble, believing in a path of faith. We can smile again, even through our despair, knowing that humor creates the distance for us to see. Storytelling becomes an act of reciprocity, a compassionate gesture toward "an ecology of mind" where we see and believe in the interconnectedness of life.

Laura Simms is an alchemist, a healer, a scholar of world literature, and a spiritual practitioner within the Buddhist tradition, who understands that the power of story is the power to believe in our own capacity to change the world. Above all, she is a seer. Her voice becomes a map to secret landscapes of desire, fear, and beauty. She knows that story is the umbilical cord between the past, present and future, it keeps things known. When a story is told it becomes the conscience of the community and we become accountable for that knowledge which has been shared. Laura Simms has been my teacher, instructing me over and over again, it is story that bypasses rhetoric and pierces the heart.

In this collection of stories, *The Robe of Love,* Laura has chosen to take us on a journey of the heart. It is not a simple path, nor is it an altogether comfortable one, but it is a path of inquiry, discovery and truth.

When the youngest daughter of the merchant asks her father to bring her the "Caftan El Hub" or "The Robe of Love," he asks her what it looks like.

"I do not know." she says. "I seek my heart's desire."

A wise woman had told her in the market, "Few seek their heart's desire, and fewer find it."

The merchant listens to his daughter and makes a vow to find "The Robe of Love."

One can never know what love will look like or what form it will take. We can only trust that when it does come, we will recognize it and have the courage to embrace the love that is ours to hold in all its beauty and terror.

Each of these fourteen stories is a passage to love with its own perils and triumphs, disappointments and miracles. Each tale is a symbolic map we can unroll and study with all its hints and clues as to how we might dare to enter and re-enter our own territories of the heart.

And each story requires its own patience and attention. I urge you to read one story at a time, outloud, to someone you love and surround it with space, allowing it to fully flower in your presence. Sit with it. Sleep on it. Hold it in your hand as a talisman. And then read it again and see what understanding comes.

It is in the power of story to remind us what we have forgotten, what we need to remember to restore our hearts. This is the bravery of Laura Simms.

She is fearless with her voice on the page and in the world. Do not underestimate the force of these tales that she has rendered in the simple, bare bones of language. They are the dreams of lovers that have inspired revolutions.

—*Terry Tempest Williams*

Introduction

You do not have to be good.
You do not have to walk on your knees
for a hundred miles through the desert, repenting.
You only have to let the soft animal of your body love
what it loves.

—Mary Oliver

I chose to write the love stories that I tell in performance. Each tale explores an aspect of longing and love. These tales come from throughout the world, from different times in history, and were told in courts, markets, in homes and on horseback. The origin of the essences of each tale is impossible to trace. Yet the narratives wear the mask or the costume of the culture and landscape from where they took shape, the taste of the translator who recomposed them on the page, and my own retelling.

The stories are not instructions "about" love. Nor are the characters and events of the stories where love is found. It is not a manual about how to fall in love or how to avoid the pitfalls of romance, disappointment and fate. Rather, love is what breaks open within the reader as the stories come to life in the invisible chambers of the heart. Love is what is always waiting within us to ignite into the fire of longing for union, or to uncover our inherent well of unconditional awareness that opens into bliss.

The unspoken work of a story is to uncover and arouse this longing. The storyteller is the guide on the ceaseless playful journey inward to bring love out of hiding. The stories are incomplete without the reader.

The content, or *outer story,* narrates the seductions and meetings, terrors and unions, disappointments and celebrations of the characters in each tale as if they existed. But these characters are not real. The real story is the *inner story* that is the tale each of us creates in the special bond between word, imagining and heart. This psychological enactment engages us in the guise of the story, but arises in the unseen spaces between bone and skin. The tales are old and have been retold for thousands of years, yet they are never outdated. For this reason, they manifest always in the present. They were also never meant for children only.

There is another story that occurs. The *secret love story* with no words or plot that is experienced and cannot be explained. As our attention is enthralled by the unfolding details of what is happening, a subterranean stream of timelessness, a fathomless ocean of passion without attachment, a communal mystery, is felt. If sought in words or image, it alludes us. This is the source of unconditional love. Such can be the effect of the physical and ephemeral nature of a book of love stories.

Reading a story is refreshing because it distracts us from the stories that haunt our everyday lives, which keep us from remembering the constant presence of love. Regardless of our beliefs or opinions, in the listening we rest in the nourishing possibility of such presence.

Scheherazhade knew that her stories were more powerful than the sword a King held over her head. The King's inner world was transformed 1001 times into a universe of listening. His habitual stories of mistrust and violence were held in abeyance by the trick of the storyteller. As he became each tale each night, thinking it was a narrative about another, his own capacity for loving and empathy, buried beneath his fear and lust for power, was unearthed and transmuted into love.

My wish is that these stories open the inner eye of each reader. Like the woman in a story whose windblown veil reveals a face that cannot be forgotten once seen, I offer these tales as an irresistible glance. So the reader becomes the lover, the seeker, the fool, longings' ceaseless companion, and the warrior of the heart who retells stories to enliven the world. ♥

The beloved is all, the lover just a veil.

The beloved is living, the lover a dead thing.

If Love witholds its strengthening care,

The lover is left like a bird without wings.

How will I be awake and aware

If the light of the Beloved is absent?

Love wills that this Word be brought forth.

If you find the mirror of the heart dull,

The rust has not been cleared from its face.

—*Rumi*

[I, 34]

The Mistress of Disguise

A TALE FROM THE CAUCASUS

A handsome prince, who lived in a fortified town by the sea, was told by the elders of his Kingdom that it was time for him to marry. Obediently, he dressed in armor, saddled his horse, and went in search of a bride. He traveled from palace to palace and cottage to cottage, but to no avail. She, who he sought, he could not find.

One day, however, he came to a castle where there lived a young woman more beautiful than any he had ever seen. Instantly, on seeing her, he fell in love with her. The prince asked the maiden to marry him, and she agreed.

As was the custom, he rode home with her on the back of his horse. The night of their arrival in the fortified town, they were married. The festivities went on for two weeks, both night and day. The couple had barely time to get to know one another. When the celebrations were ended, the prince was informed that it was customary for the new groom to set out on a year-long journey, leaving his new wife at home, to see the rest of the known world.

Beautiful Helena, for that was her name, was surprised and

dismayed. It was difficult for the prince to tear himself away, but custom proceeded matters of the heart. And he left.

Beautiful Helena was lonely. After two months a Turkish merchant arrived in a boat laden with treasures and she had him invited to the palace to exhibit his wares. The merchant was unusually handsome and his goods were rare silks, carved silver goblets, brocades and precious stones from exotic places. Everyone who came to the market left speaking more about the elegance and charm of the merchant than the treasures he displayed for sale.

Helena was delighted with him as well, and invited him often to her rooms for dinner and conversations. The merchant was equally attracted to Helena. Their loneliness was softened by the friendship they shared. As the months passed, the merchant did not return to the sea, and their friendship grew more and more intimate.

The two lovers hardly noticed time. When suddenly they realized that the prince would return within days, they were miserable. Helena and the merchant did not want to part.

One of the handmaidens of the princess pitied them, for she realized what they shared was true love and she made a plan. She whispered to the merchant as he gathered his belongings to leave, "I cannot stand to see you suffer. It is rare for one to find true love in this world. Tomorrow, near the shore where the sea is screened by thick bushes, wait for the princess. I will arrange for her to bathe in that place."

For a few moments the merchant objected. But in less time, he agreed. The next day the handmaiden convinced the princess that the cold seawater would relieve her sorrow, and that she could see the merchant's boat set sail. Undressing, the sorrowful princess walked into the water.

Suddenly, the merchant appeared in a small wooden boat. The princess at first refused and wept. But within seconds, she climbed willingly into the boat forsaking duty for the truth of her heart.

The handmaiden locked herself into Helena's rooms for three days so no one would suspect that the princess was gone until they were far out to sea. On the fourth morning the handmaiden began to scream and tear at her hair shouting, "The princess has been kidnapped while she slept in the night."

2

When, at last, the prince arrived home, the elders, family, courtiers and guests distracted him with food and wine. No one wanted to tell him about his missing wife. However, the prince knew something was wrong. He demanded to see Helena. He was informed. He asked for the strange tale of her disappearance to be retold a hundred times. The news struck him like lightening blinds an eye, like an arrow pierces the flesh. He set out from his desolate palace to find his abducted wife.

The prince searched throughout his kingdom. No one had seen her and he could not find her. He went to his old tutor, the one who had taken care of him as a child and who guided him in all matters.

The old man scolded the prince, "Only a fool would hide the princess in your country. Your intelligence is not as developed as your courage. You should search on the other side of the sea. Whether it is one year or two years, you must travel until you find her, and bring her back."

So, the prince ordered a ship prepared and he set off. After some time he saw mountains in the distance, and a ship sailing toward his own.

On the deck of the ship stood an elegant youth wearing a cloak of mail with a quiver over one shoulder. He held a bow in one hand and wore a sword on his other side. On his head shone a steel helmet reflecting sea and sun.

The prince was dressed in the same fashion, but his costume was distinguished as royalty by a large brooch over his heart. The young man in respect climbed onto the deck of the prince's ship to greet him.

"Where are you traveling?" inquired the youth.

The Prince told the story of his search.

The young man asked, "Why do you travel without a friend? You have no one to share the dangers of your journey, or to converse with through idle hours at sea."

The Prince answered, "I have no companion."

"I will be your friend," said the youth.

Thus, they traveled together seeking news of Helena, the Beautiful. No one seemed to have heard of a merchant who stole away a princess and the Prince said to his companion, "I am afraid I will never find her."

The young man said, "You will never find her dressed as

a prince. It is best to seek her in a disguise. I know a lot about disguises. Dress as a beggar and no one will fear to talk to you."

The prince took his good advice. He put on ragged clothes, leaned on a pilgrim's staff, and walked as if his back was curved from years of hard labor.

Within three days, the prince/beggar was told about a large house owned by a merchant in which there lived the most beautiful woman in the world.

In the second story of the house, the beggar found Beautiful Helena reclining on a brocaded couch. She recognized him at once and in a harsh voice, feigning disgust, ordered her servants, "Sweep out that filthy beggar as you do the trash from this house!"

"What should I do now? She does not recognize me," said the Prince to his friend.

The companion said, "Take off your beggar's robes and put on your royal clothes. Arm yourself with a sword and take back your wife with force."

The words of his friend matched his understanding and his training and the prince dressed himself for battle. He burst into the merchant's house and climbed the stairs to cut off the heads of Helena's servants. He dragged her screaming and crying from the house.

As the prince rowed the small wooden boat with his captured wife beside him toward the ship, he recognized that she looked longingly back toward the merchant's house. She cared nothing for him. And the prince recognized that he did not know Helena who sat beside him. He felt no love for her at all.

The companion suggested, "Since she is not your true love, then you can either send her back in the wooden boat by herself and it is her destiny whether she returns alive to the merchant or not. Or, you can slice her in two with your sword and we will each take a half and throw it into the sea."

The prince made one choice unbeknownst to the storyteller and thus unbeknownst to my listeners as well. But, he returned to his fortified town alone with his new companion.

As they came near the walled city, the young man said, "I will now return to my own ship and hope that we will meet again." Then added, "If you still seek true love without finding it, my friend, then perhaps you should travel over seven mountain ranges to a stone castle where the seven Baraghun Brothers live with their warrior sister. Perhaps, she is your true love." The prince thanked him for his friendship.

They parted and the Prince returned home.

One year later, lonely, and haunted by the parting words of his friend, the prince traveled over seven mountain ranges. He found the stone palace of the Baraghun warrior Brothers. Seven fierce warriors were seated on seven iron thrones wearing swords and metal boots, and helmets adorned with the tails of wolves.

Their voices bellowed loudly, shattering the silence of their castle, "What brings you here?"

The prince answered, "I was told that your sister is my true love."

The seven brothers shook with laughter. "She is so fierce that we don't go in her room for fear of her."

"I think she may be my true beloved," revealed the prince.

The youngest and least fierce of the warrior brothers said, "I will open the door and risk my life just to see what she does at the sight of you!" And the seventh brother pushed open a thick iron door.

The sister of the seven brothers sat on a tall silver throne. She was wearing layers of animal skins and armor. She wore metal boots, and had three swords hanging from her belt. On her head she wore a copper helmet with tails of fox and marmot, wild dog and lynx. She cried out in a voice like thunder rattling in a mountain cave, "WHAT ARE YOU DOING HERE?"

The prince, not daring to step over the threshold said, "I think you are my true love."

"WHAT DO YOU WANT?" she shouted.

"I want to marry you." he answered.

"WHAT DO YOU WANT?" she screeched.

"I think I want to marry you," he repeated.

Her shoulders shook as she answered, "ALL RIGHT."

That night there was a wedding in the stone castle. She sat at her own table devouring everything. The prince barely ate. He drank as much wine as he could, terrified of his wedding night.

However, when he and his wife got into bed, he with his wedding cloak and she with three layers of skin and a vest of armor, she turned her back and said, "I AM TIRED." The prince was relieved and distressed. He couldn't sleep.

During the night, the prince heard his wife move toward the edge of the bed. She moved silently until she stood on the cold stone floor. He watched as she dressed herself for battle in layer upon layer of animal skins and iron mail. Then she placed an iron helmet over her head and attached six arrows with banners of seven colors. She put on her metal boots and left the room.

The prince stealthily climbed from the bed, put on armor and helmet and followed behind her unseen. She took a horse from the stables and rode out of the castle walls. The prince leaped upon his own horse and followed in the distance.

As the princess rode, armies gathered behind her from every direction. She rode before them all. The prince rode beside one man and inquired, "Where are you going tonight?"

"We ride behind our general. Tonight's battle decides all others. If she is victorious, then our war is come to an end. And if we lose, we give up our entire country," said the soldier.

The prince rode on beside the soldier. He watched his wife from a distance as she organized her armies with the skill of an excellent general. Then she too rode into battle against the giant army. Hour after hour the battle raged and the prince never took his eyes off his wife. As a strategist she excelled. Her art with the sword and the bow was unequalled.

However, almost at dawn, the battle shifted and his wife's army seemed to lose its strength and focus. Suddenly she was surrounded by enemy and fighting for her life alone. The prince put down his visor and rode down to fight beside his bride. With his help she defeated the enemy, but in battle the prince's hand was cut.

The general took a red silk scarf from beneath her armor and wrapped his wound. At that moment, the prince realized he should ride home quickly because it was necessary to be in bed before his wife. He turned and rode away with all speed.

In bed, he tried to quiet his breath, his body worn weary from battle. But the warrior princess did not notice, for she too was weary and lay beside him, her heart beating heavily and her body weary. They both sank into a deep sleep.

In the morning they awoke at the same moment. Now, without her armor and skins of beasts, the princess turned toward him. The prince was startled by her beauty. And, aroused by unforeseen passion he reached out for his wife. She looked up and their eyes met. The prince stared into her eyes, at her cheeks, at her lips, at the curve of her dark eyes, when she noticed the red scarf.

"Where were you last night?" she asked.

He said, "I was with you." He asked, "Do you do this every night?"

"Not any more. There is no more need for battle."

She added "You were a true companion."

"I have had only had one friend," answered the prince as he looked deeply into her eyes. And then he recognized her. She was the one who had been his true companion. Then they were truly wed without disguise, without constraint.

When they made love the walls of the fortified city crumbled like dust into the sea and her mountain castle and his seaside palace became one. ❦

7

THE TEMPTRESS

So you think you've been alive!

I'll make your pores open like fish mouths.

When you hear banging pipes —

that'll be your blood.

Light will soothe your eyes like a silk shawl

Gravity will stab your heel like a thorn.

Your shoulder blades will cry for wings.

And you think you are alive!

Well, falling dust will deafen you!

Your eyebrows will be burning gashes

and you will swear your memory began

at the birth of time.

—*Nina Cassian*

The Garden Woman

A Georgian tale

A wealthy young man owned a beautiful house with a well-tended garden. He did not like to work, so he hired a gardener to keep the rows of flowers and vegetables neat. Every evening, at the same time before the sun set, the young man went to sit on a marble bench and admire his plants.

One evening he saw a crumpled piece of paper lying among his lovely flowers. He ordered the gardener to remove "the mess" and he returned to his house.

The gardener lifted up a dried onion and began to open the skins. In the middle was a piece of paper with words delicately printed on it. The gardener could not read, so he threw away the paper with the dried onion.

The next morning, when the gardener came to work, he saw a woman walking back and forth between the rows of vegetables and flowers. She was dressed in leaves and petals, adorned with stalks and dangling roots. She was beautiful. The gardener was delighted.

That evening when the young man returned to his bench, he too saw the Garden Woman. Her beauty enchanted him. For the first time in his life, the idea of getting married entered his mind. He leaped over the rows of flowers and plants calling out to her, "Who are you? What is your name?"

The Garden Woman stopped walking, stood arms akimbo, and answered, "My name is Leek. I am wearing a fennel belt and I am a Garden Woman."

The young man was horrified. "I could never marry a woman named Leek!" and abruptly turned and left the garden.

Within weeks he had met a woman and married. He brought his bride home and did not return to view his garden for several days. The Garden Woman was distressed. Who can explain the female heart?

She called to the gardener, who adored her, and asked, "Could you milk twelve doe? Warm the milk in a bathtub placed in the middle of the garden. I feel I need to bathe." The gardener, who would have done anything for her, agreed. The next day he climbed up the mountain, into the forest, and milked twelve doe. He placed the heated milk into a bathtub placed in the middle of the garden for her to bathe.

That evening, the young man came again to admire his garden. As he sat down, the Garden Woman removed her clothing of leaves and petals and stepped naked into the heated milk. The young man had never seen anything so remarkable. He rushed home to his bride and told her about the beautiful naked woman in the garden taking a bath in hot milk. She remarked, "That is very interesting."

The next morning, the wife ordered the gardener to move the bathtub to the front of the house and fill it with the boiled milk of twelve cows. The gardener was hired to obey his master's whims, so he agreed.

That evening as the new husband set off for his garden, his bride called out, "Come, look." She took off her clothes and stepped into the boiling milk.

Unfortunately, she boiled to death.

Days later, the widower remembered his garden. He went to his marble bench at the usual hour, and there walking up and down the aisles of flowers was the Garden Woman. Again, he had a desire to get married. He jumped over the rows of plants and lettuce, and called out, "Please. What is your name? You must be called Carnation, Dahlia, Tulip, Lilly, or Rose?"

Hands on her hips, the Garden Woman stood still and answered, "I told you. My name is Leek. I am wearing a belt made of fennel. I am a Garden Woman."

The young man was offended. He said to her, "I could never marry a woman named Leek!"

He went home and within days was married again. The Garden Woman missed him. She asked the gardener to find her a wooden loom, a wooden shuttle, and a little silver knife. The Gardener was happy to do whatever the Garden Woman asked without question.

"Please place the loom, the shuttle and the knife on the roof of his house this evening."

When it was dark the Garden Woman climbed up a ladder to the roof and began to weave and sing. The young man saw her from his window. He woke his bride, saying, "There is something remarkable occurring on our roof." She looked at the beautiful woman dressed in leaves, weaving on the wooden loom and answered, "That is interesting."

At that moment the Garden Woman pretended that the shuttle fell from her hands. She took out the silver knife, cut off her nose, and said to her nose, "Please bring me back the shuttle."

The nose soared down, lifted up the shuttle, and brought it back to the Garden Woman. She put the nose back on her face and continued weaving.

The young man remarked, "That was astonishing. That was enchanting!"

The new wife said nothing. But the next day ordered the gardener to keep the loom on the roof. Scratching his head, the gardener thought, "What is it with these women?"

That night the new wife sat on the roof weaving and singing. The young man was pleased. When he stretched his head out the window to get a better look, she feigned dropping the shuttle. Then she took the silver knife, cut off her nose and sent it after the shuttle.

Unfortunately, she bled to death.

Several evenings later the young man returned to his marble bench to look at his garden. The Garden Woman was walking back and forth among the growing things. He was again smitten with an uncanny desire to get married.

"Who are you? What is your name? You must be called Narcissus, Iris, Gardenia, or Orchid?" He called to her leaping over the rows of flowers and vegetables.

She said, "I have told you already twice. My name is Leek. I am wearing a belt of fennel and I am a Garden Woman."

This time the young man heard her words and raced up the side of the mountain. He threw off his clothes and bled the neck of a wild pig to cover himself in blood. Then he rolled his body in the mud and ran down to the garden again.

The young man lay down on the earth between flowers and vegetables and said, "Please tell me who you are?"

She answered, "You know who I am. My name is Leek. I am wearing a belt made of fennel. I am a Garden Woman. Get up. Go home and wash yourself. Get dressed and let's get married."

And that is what they did. ❦

Diarmud's Longing

AN IRISH TALE

Diarmud, whose name means "no envy," was one of the Fianna, a band of supernatural warrior hunters who were great bards. Diarmud was both blessed and cursed by love. A goddess placed a love-spot on his forehead, so that any woman who looked at him would fall in love with him. It was for this reason that Diarmud always wore a bandana.

Each day of every winter, the Fianna, led by the chief called Finn McCoul, hunted. At night they slept together in a house warmed by a central fire.

One bitter midnight, when the snow was thick and the wind furious, there was a knock at the door. Finn went to see who it was.

Outside, drenched and miserable, stood a hideous woman. Her face was strained with filth and age. Her wet knotted hair hung to her knees. Her clothing, insufficient for the cold, was torn and stinking.

Finn asked disgusted, "What do you want?"

She screeched her words, "Please let me come into the house and rest beneath the corner of your cloak."

Finn said, "No!" and turned away. The woman shrieked.

So, Oissin, Finn's son, went to the door. She begged, "Please let me enter and lay down beneath the corner of your cloak."

He answered, "No!"

Again, she screamed, hurtling her pain like a jagged knife.

Diarmud went to the door and took pity on her. He said, holding his breath against her smell, "Come rest yourself beneath the corner of my cloak."

She followed behind him. It was as if the ghost of the smell of the garbage of the world, the stench of a thousand rotting fish, came inside with her. She lay down on the floor hugging the corner of his cloak. When she was rested, she whispered in a hoarse whine, "Can I sit beside the fire? I am so cold."

Diarmud could not refuse. But, when he took her to the hearth, the other men fled to the corners of the room.

She warmed herself and begged, "Couldn't I just lay beneath the covers of your blanket?"

Diarmud reluctantly agreed. Rushing to the bed he made a fold down the center of the sheet so she would know her side. The Fianna thought him mad.

The hag fell into a deep sleep. Diarmud lay awake, disturbed. In the middle of the night, curious, he turned to look at her face, this near demon that he had pitied and taken into his bed. He was astonished to see the most lovely woman asleep beside him. Gone were her stink and her age and her ugliness. Quietly, he unfolded the sheet that separated them.

She opened her eyes, "Diarmud. I have traveled across sea and over the world for seven years in search of someone who would comfort me. No one but you would take me in as I was. For this I will give you whatever you have longed for."

Diarmud's insides were a small fire gone burning. Her beauty and the sound of her voice tore off the shell of his heart, made it bare and raw and open.

He blurted out, "I have always desired a house on the hill beside this place. A greyhound with three new pups. And a woman of my own."

She smiled, "Diarmud, all that you ask will be yours." He added, "But I want no other woman than you." She answered gently, "I am yours."

When Diarmud lifted his arm to embrace her, she touched him. He fell into a deep sleep.

In the morning she was gone from the bed. But there was the house on the hill, and his beloved at the door with the greyhound and her pups. Diarmud raced up the hill and embraced her. For seven days and seven nights they never left their bed, and Diarmud felt a comfort he had never known before.

On the eighth morning she remarked, "Don't you miss the company of men?" Diarmud admitted that he did not. She urged him up and sent him to spend his time with the Fianna.

"And who will care for the dogs?" he asked.

"I will take care of the dogs, and the house, and myself."

Awkwardly Diarmud asked, "And you will be here when I return?"

To this she said, "I will remain with you for the rest of your life as long as you never mention three times how it was I looked when you first saw me."

Diarmud said, "I have forgotten already."

That afternoon Finn passed by the house in hopes of seeing Diarmud's love. He was sorry that he didn't have the courage to let her in their lodge the first night. She gladly invited him in for a glass of wine, and asked if there was anything he desired. Finn asked for one of the greyhound pups and she gave it.

Soon Diarmud returned home. The mother dog rushed to the door and yelped once as any mother cries when she loses a child. When Diarmud heard that his beloved had given away one of the pups, Diarmud raged. "You gave away what I love, when I took you in looking like a filthy stinking hag!"

Then he remembered his vow and apologized.

She said, "I am sorry as well." And they returned to their lovemaking.

But the next afternoon it happened again that one of the Fianna came to visit her and requested one of Diarmud's pups. When he returned later that day, the greyhound howled twice for her loss and again Diarmud could not control his anger.

"How could you give away what is mine when I accepted you the way you looked and smelled the first night?" Again,

15

he recalled his promise and was sorry.

However, on the third day when the dog howled three times, Diarmud spit with fury and called out, "You were ugly and stinking, wench, and I let you sleep beside me?" In that instant, the woman he loved disappeared. The house vanished in thin air. Diarmud turned to rush after her, but a terrible weariness fell over him and he tumbled to the earth asleep.

In the morning, he awoke and ran down the hill. The greyhound's body lay dead on the ground. He picked up the corpse and set it over his shoulders like a cloak.

No one had seen her, except for a farmer who was turning the dry ground at the top of a hill. "She sailed away on a small boat that came to the shore."

Seeing a small boat out to sea, Diarmud leaned on his spear and catapulted himself onto its deck. It was empty except for a fisherman who said not a word and rowed further away from his home to a desolate island.

After days of waiting, a raft appeared in the distance. Again, with the corpse of the dog on his shoulders, Diarmud thrust himself over the water by the curve of his spear and alighted on the raft. The ferryman said, "She is the daughter of the King of the Waves beneath the Sea, and I took her to the middle of the ocean. She was sick and weak with disappointment."

Diarmud begged, "Can you take me there? I am the cause of her sorrow."

The ferryman rowed him to the middle of the ocean and pointing into the sea, held the raft firm as Diarmud dove beneath the waves.

The world below was an endless desert of sand. Diarmud saw three drops of blood, and thinking they were from the greyhound took them up in a cloth and placed them in his pocket. He wandered, searching for his wife, until he saw a young girl weeping knee-deep in reeds, frantically trying to gather them. He asked her the way to the daughter of the King of the Sea and she cried out, never stopping her ceaseless pulling and tossing of the reeds, "The princess is ill and dying. The only comfort she finds is to rest in these reeds. I gather them. I gather them. I cannot stop."

Diarmud said, "I am the one who has betrayed her. Take

me to her please."

The girl said, "Lie down in these reeds and I will carry you."

He said, "I am too large a man."

But she lay the reeds on the sand and ordered him to lie down. She wrapped him in the long grass and easily lifted him onto her shoulders and carried him to the palace where his beloved lay beneath layers of silk and reeds.

She raised her head and said, "Diarmud, you have come."

He fell to his knees, touching her hand. "How can I heal you?"

"Many men have tried but none have succeeded. It is impossible."

"I would give my life to see you healthy again," said Diarmud.

"At the end of this world there is a river that is as tiny as a thin blade of grass and as vast as the sky. It is inconceivable and no one can cross it. On the other side is an island where there lives a King who has stolen my golden cup. If you mix healing waters from the well at the shore of my world and three drops of my blood in that cup, I will be healed."

"I have the three drops of your blood." He realized that she and the greyhound were one.

Diarmud pulled himself away from her and left immediately. He traveled until he arrived at the end of her world, by the shore of an inconceivable river. What she said was true. There was no way that he could cross it. Diarmud sat on the sand and cried.

Suddenly, a red dwarf leapt like a fish from beneath the water and held out the palm of his hand. Placing one foot on the dwarf's palm, Diarmad was tossed onto the island. The dwarf followed behind him saying, "I will accompany you."

Diarmud paid no heed to the little man because his mind was set on his task. He saw one hundred thousand huge armed warriors arise and surround a palace in the middle of the island. Diarmud aroused his battle rage, growing three times his size.

Crying out as if his voice could utter a thousand syllables at once, he attacked the terrible army. He battled for five hours and defeated every single man. Then, another two hundred thousand warriors appeared and attacked

Diarmud. Again, infused with his supernatural rage and his battle passion, Diarmud killed them all. The island was strewn with limbs and blood.

The King of the island, astonished and angry, walked toward Diarmud. "Who are you who has destroyed my entire army?"

"My name is Diarmud and I have come to retrieve the golden cup that will heal my beloved."

"If you would have told me your name in the first place, all of this blood could have been avoided. For the past seven years there has been a prophecy that only a warrior named Diarmud could receive the cup. Now take it and be gone."

Diarmud asked, "Can this vessel filled with sacred waters heal?"

"How should I know?" answered the King who gave him the cup and returned to his palace.

Diarmud relaxed his warrior's rage, and cup in hand walked swiftly to the shore. Seeing the inconceivable waters he remembered that he had no way to cross. The dwarf appeared behind him. "I am still here," called out the dwarf and Diarmud turned.

"Aren't you curious to know who I am?" inquired the little red man.

"Later. I haven't the time now to talk," said Diarmud.

However, the dwarf insisted, and Diarmud listened. "I come from another world and I only help those who burn with the desire to aid another."

Then the red dwarf again held out the flat palm of his hand. The warrior placed one foot on it and the dwarf tossed him to the other side.

The dwarf showed him the healing well and Diarmud filled the cup with its water and the three drops of blood and began to walk toward the palace of the daughter of the King of the Waves Beneath the Sea.

Diarmud looked up to see the woman walking toward him. Her pale skin and weary body brought tears to his eyes. She moved slowly covered with a heavy cloak. As she came near, the red dwarf tapped him on the shoulder saying, "I forgot to tell you something."

Diarmud whispered, "It can wait."

But the dwarf insisted.

"What is it then?" he demanded.

I forgot to explain that when she drinks the first drop her skin will shine. When she drinks the second her strength and health will return. And when she drinks the third drop the love will be gone from you. She will know it. Do not pretend."

"It cannot be," said Diarmud.

"It is true," said the dwarf. "Tonight the King will celebrate the return of her health and your victory. He will offer you gifts, but ask only for a ship to sail back to your world." The dwarf dove back into the river and disappeared.

Then, she, the one he loved, stood beside Diarmud saying, "Beloved, you have brought me the cup that heals. You have done what no man before you could."

Diarmud's heart ached as he gave her the cup. With the first sip, color returned to her cheeks. With the second, she stood tall and smiled. And with the third the love disappeared from Diarmud. She saw it and turned away.

That night there was a great feast in the palace and the King offered the warrior a thousand gifts, but he asked only for a ship to return to his world.

And when Diarmud sailed home, the Fianna, and all the people of Ireland, welcomed him back joyfully. Beneath the sea, the daughter of the King held the golden cup that was her own, and she was healed. ❦

I sleep, but my heart is awake.

— Song of Songs

The Golden Tree

A JEWISH TALE FROM INDIA

An impetuous King had four wives. There was one wife who he favored. She was kind, intelligent, challenging and beautiful. The three other wives were jealous of the time he spent with her. Over the years, they connived and complained, and finally convinced the King that the fourth wife was the source of all the troubles in the kingdom. One morning, when the favored wife refused to agree with the King, he banished her saying, "Your ill will is the cause of all my problems. And, you have not born me a child after years of marriage!"

The Queen knew well the devious root of the King's change of heart. Without a word, she left the palace. Disguised as a beggar, she journeyed until she arrived in India. There she found a small cottage in a forest and lived a simple life.

One night she dreamed of a magnificent Golden Tree. In the morning, she realized that she was pregnant. However, she sent no word to her husband, the King.

That same night the King also dreamed of the Golden

Tree. The next morning he could not stop thinking of the wife whom he had banished. Realizing his mistake, he set out to find her and ask for her forgiveness.

He traveled following the merchants who said they had seen the woman he described. He too arrived in India. But he could not find his wife. Finally, he sought the advice of a sage. No disguise could hide her true beauty. The wise sage did not tell him how to find her. Instead, he advised the King to find the Golden Tree he had seen in his dream. "Then you will find your true love," said the sage.

His journey was arduous and long. The King's feet were hardened, his robes were torn to shreds and a beard grew from his chin. But, at last, in the middle of a boiling lake, he saw an island on which grew the Golden Tree.

He risked his life and crossed the fiery water and took a single branch of the tree. He saw his wife's face reflected, as if in a mirror, on every leaf. He wept until his heart was cleansed of selfishness and the boiling water around him was cool and still. Then, soon afterward, he entered a forest he had not seen before. He came upon the cottage of his wife. She recognized him instantly for she had loved him with all of her heart. She saw the branch of the Golden Tree she had dreamed of in his hands. Yet, uncertain of the nature of his visit, the Queen let her seven-year-old son stay unseen. When she opened the door, he knew her as well.

The King asked for her forgiveness. They told each other their tales, and she gladly forgave him.

She then introduced her husband to their child. The Queen, the King and the Prince returned home. The gold branch was planted in the royal garden and grew as a reminder of their love. The three other queens were banished. They set off on their journeys. May they too be tempered by love. ❦

Sandalwood Leaves

A TALE RETOLD, FROM PERSIA

T here were once two young men, as different as day
and night, who were the best of friends. One's per-
sonality was defined by his extreme kindness and the
other was known for his unrelenting selfishness. The
young man who was kind was named Kheyr, which
translates as "Good." The other young man without kind-
ness was named Sharr, which means "Evil." They decided to
travel together across a desert to a distant market.

As they traveled, they suffered from the same heat. Both
drank from a single water pouch. The oasis seemed to
allude them.

"Do not worry," Sharr reassured his friend, "I know this
desert well. We will find water tomorrow." He had an extra
water pouch hidden beneath his coat, and when they
stopped to sleep he stayed awake and quenched his thirst.

Kheyr complained bitterly, "I am sure we will die before we
find water. My friend, how is it that you do not complain?"

When they were not far from the oasis, Kheyr's suffering
made him too weak to continue. Sharr said, "I do not com-
plain because I drink water every night while you sleep." He

showed the water pouch to his friend.

Kheyr begged, "Please let me have a drop of water."

Sharr said, "What will you give me for this drop of water?"

Realizing that greed had overtaken his friend's mind, Kheyr took the two priceless rubies that he had carried to sell in the market from his pocket. He gave them to his friend.

"Rubies can be bought and sold in the market. If you want to give me something of value, give me your two eyes," demanded Sharr.

Kheyr wept. He pleaded with his friend to not engage in such evil, but to no avail. Then he said, "What use are my eyes when I am dead?" Taking a knife, he cut out his own eyes and gave them to his friend.

Sharr threw Kheyr's eyes in the sand and left him to die. He took the two rubies and walked to the nearby oasis.

Kheyr lay in agony. His painful moans echoed in the devouring silence of sand and wind. The anguish he felt in his heart was more severe than the pain he experienced in his mutilated body.

Not far from where he lay, a Kurdish chief had set up his tents for the night. He sent his daughter to get water from the oasis and as she returned, she heard the pitiful cries of a man. She found Kheyr blinded and half dead. Then she saw his two eyes lying in the sand. Washing them with water, she wrapped the eyes in cloth and gave Kheyr some water.

The Chieftain's daughter gathered leaves known for their healing properties from a sandalwood tree. She pounded the leaves and made a salve. She set Kheyr's eyes back in place, and placed layer upon layer of sandalwood salve over his face, then covered his skin with bandages of the softest cotton. She sat by his side day and night to care for him.

When Kheyr awoke he was surprised to discover that he was alive. His eyes remained bound in cloth. He was certain that he was blind. But his heart, mind and voice were unharmed. The Kurdish princess delighted in his conversation. When he told his terrible tale, the Chieftain swore that if he should ever find this man named Sharr, he would kill him in vengence.

Kheyr and the Kurdish princess fell in love, drawn together by the beauty of their voices and the truth of their words. As the weeks passed, they promised that they would never be separated. Kheyr asked for her hand in marriage.

The princess asked her father if she could marry the blind man whose kindness matched her own. The Chieftain, who had grown to love him like a son, agreed.

On the morning of the wedding, Kheyr's bandages were unwound. His eyes were healed. "I can see again as a result of love and the leaves of the sandalwood tree," he said. He recognized that the loveliness of his beloved was equal to the goodness of her heart. "All beauty is in the inner eyes of those that truly see," he said. Khyer felt himself rewarded with a gift far more precious than rubies or his own sight.

The wedding lasted for seven days and seven nights. There was dancing and singing, storytelling and feasting. Kheyr came to know the pleasures of the shared life of the Kurdish tribe's people. Yet he longed to see his own city, and one day announced that he would like to return home with his new bride. The Kurdish Chieftain gave him horses, servants and gifts and wished them good luck. They promised to meet each year.

As they traveled from their camp in the desert, they could not find their way back to his home. They wandered until they arrived at the walls of an unfamiliar city where everyone seemed cloaked in sorrow. They were told that the daughter of the King suffered from a strange illness and could not speak or walk. The Kurdish woman offered to heal her. Kheyr and his wife gathered leaves of the sandalwood tree and ground it into a salve. They lay it on the body of the young girl and sat beside her. Who can say which healed the most, the medicine of the plants, or the medicine of love?

But within three days the young princess was healed. The King said that he had never had a son, "Will you not stay here and become the King of my country when I die? I will share all my wealth with you. My young daughter is promised to a King of another country and there will be no one to rule. I have never met a man or a woman of such generosity." Because they had given up hope of returning to Kheyr's city, they agreed.

On the death of the old King, Kheyr became the King of this wealthy and abundant country. The new rulers brought even greater harmony to the kingdom and everyone loved them. The years passed quickly. In time, the Kurdish Chieftain came to live in the city as well.

One day as the King was standing at the window, he heard the voice of a merchant boasting in the market. Recognizing the voice, he asked that the merchant be brought before him. Robed in audacious colors and covered with jewels, an arrogant merchant displayed his goods before the King. "I sell the rarest jewels to be found in any of the world's markets."

"I know something of your capacities," said the King.

And the merchant puffed up his chest, "Yes, my reputation is as great as my talents."

"What is your name?"

"My name is Morbesharr," said the man.

"And my name is Kheyr. I am the one whose eyes you demanded, and whose rubies you stole, and whose body you left in the desert to die."

Immediately Sharr threw himself to the ground and beat his head against the marble floor. "Your majesty I have regretted that day every day of my life, and I beg you for forgiveness." Then he begged, "Please do not kill me. I did not know what I was doing."

The King pitied his friend, whose fortune was small compared to his own.

The King said, "I will not kill you. But you will live as a beggar outside the gates of this kingdom in order to learn humility."

The merchant was divested of his robes and led outside the gates of the kingdom dressed as a beggar.

One day the Kurdish Chieftain recognized the beggar. Fulfilling his promise of revenge, he killed Sharr.

Khyer wept when he heard of his friend's death. He had the body buried outside the oasis where he had lost his eyes. He kept the rubies so he would not forget his friend. Every year, dressed in sandalwood-colored robes, he rode out to where Sharr was buried. He mourned the death of his friend. ❧

The Magic Drum

ADAPTED FROM AN INUIT TALE

There was once a young woman who was very beautiful. She refused to marry because she felt no man was good enough for her. Every day she sat outside of her house made of ice and skins. One day she saw a handsome man walk through the village. She thought, "This stranger is a man that I would marry." He quickly began to leave the village. Rather than watch him go, she pulled on her coat and slipped a crescent-shaped bone knife into the belt she wore, and followed him out of the village.

Never speaking, the stranger turned to warn her away. But she pursued him. He walked onto the tundra. She walked behind him. He began to run, loping like an antelope. She walked faster. He turned again to warn her away, but she followed, walking even faster.

When he came to the ice, he leaned forward, moving swiftly. The young woman stepped onto the solid white shining sea. He ran fast and she hurried behind him as the coat he wore turned to white fur and his neck bent forward toward the frozen earth. His legs grew thick. His nose expanded and became a snout, and he grew ears and paws. His coat became white fur. The man she followed became a polar bear and still she pursued him.

The bear came to a hole in the ice and dove down. The woman came to the same hole and dove after him. Her body freezing, she swam to keep up with him. There was another hole above and the bear pulled himself easily out of the water onto the ice. When the woman tried to follow, she could not climb out of the sea. She shouted, "You forgot about me." But, she heard his footsteps thump thump on the ice as he moved away.

It was too cold. She began to sink. Hundreds of tiny fish, their mouths like scissors, surrounded her and cut off the clothing that she wore. She sunk, naked, toward the bottom of the icy water. Then thousands of fish, their mouths like knives, cut off her skin and she fell lightly toward the earth, a skeleton. When her bone-feet touched the bottom of the sea, she rose up quickly, like a ball bounces back from the ground.

As a skeleton she was able to pull herself out of the hole onto the ice. She started running. Her bones were clinking and rattling. She kept thinking that perhaps she should never have followed that man. Finally, exhausted, the skeleton-woman fell onto the ice, a pile of bones, and she fell into a deep sleep.

Later she awoke clothed in thick fur skins. There was a fire burning. She was home in her own house, in her own bed. She thought, "That was a terrifying dream." Yet, when she reached out her cold hands to warm them, she saw she was still bone.

The skeleton-woman went outside to find help. No one else was in the village. She was alone.

She returned to her home and sat down outside the house as she always had. She waited for someone to find her.

After several days, two young hunters came near the house. She looked up at them, the furs falling from her skull. When they saw that she was a skeleton, the two men ran away, screaming. They rushed home and told their father about the woman made only of bones. The old man gathered up his coat, took his round drum, and went out to find her.

The skeleton-woman still sat on her wood bench outside

the door of her house, except now she kept her fur cape covering her face, so no one would be afraid.

The old man came near. He said, "Aren't you going to invite me inside? I am cold." Making certain he could not see her bone face, she led him inside where the fire lit up the room. The old man put out the flames and sat down on the floor. He said, "I will play my drum and sing. You will dance."

She said, "I cannot dance. I am only bones."

He began to play the drum and told her again to dance. The skeleton-woman lifted one foot and then another, and began to turn. At first she moved slowly rattling, afraid to swirl too quickly. But as the drumbeat entered her spirit, she turned and leaped and danced. As she felt the wind move through her bones, her skin returned. Her blood flowed and her thick black hair grew back. Her eyes glowed and she laughed as she danced.

The old man said, "That is good. Now you play the drum and I will dance."

She took the drum and the old man stood up, holding his weary back. She beat the drum in one rhythm, steady, singing as the old man began to turn. Tentative at first, then gaining strength, he leaped and turned and danced and danced until his wrinkled skin grew smooth, his eyes glowed and his white hair turned black. He danced himself young.

The skeleton woman said, "That is good."

Then the two young lovers left the house together. They carried the drum. She still had the little crescent knife in her belt. His beautiful coat was made from the pelts of a white bear. They walked to his house.

When the two young hunters saw a young man and a young woman, they inquired, "Who are you?"

The man said, "I am your old father and this is the skeleton-woman."

Terrified, the two young men chased them out of the house.

The man and the woman placed the drum on the ground. Hands clasped, smiling, they jumped into the middle of the drum and disappeared. ♣

When love rose like the sun
She had no fear;
She ran towards it
Hands open, eyes shut,
Arms held out wide
As if to catch
Its burning sphere.

— *Sally Wheeler*

Savitri

A TALE RETOLD FROM THE MAHABHARATA, INDIA

I n India, there was a King named Asvapati, which means, "Lord of Horses." He was a great ruler whose country and subjects flourished. In his kingdom, called Mudra, there was peace and wealth and happiness. However, he and his Queen had no child. So, there was no heir to the throne.

For many years, Asvapati and his wife prayed intensely for a son. Then, they repeated the mantra of the Goddess Savitri one-hundred-thousand times and asked for her aid, for she was the "stimulator of energy, the bestower of long life," and one of the consorts of the Great Lord Brahma, Lord of Knowledge.

At last, their prayers were answered and the Queen became pregnant. She gave birth to a girl. In appreciation of the Goddess they named her Savitri. As she grew up, she equaled her name. She was graceful and beautiful and she excelled in goodness and intelligence. Her accomplishments were such that no young man came to ask for her hand in marriage because they feared that she was a goddess incarnate.

Thus, one day, the King called his daughter to his court and told her to go out into the world and find a husband.

"How will I know if a man is worthy to be a King?" asked his daughter. Asvapati answered, "The man you choose must seem as good to you as you are to me. You shall know."

So, Savitri left the Kingdom of Mudra with her courtiers and a trusted minister to find herself a husband.

Many months passed. Savitri traveled far. Then, one day she returned. She was excited and sought her father. The King was sitting in his court discoursing with the sage Narada. Narada was renowned for his realizations and yogic feats. He was said to know the past, the present and the future.

"I can see from your face that you have made a choice," said her father happily.

Savitri answered, "I have found the man who will be my husband. His name is Satyavan." She paused, "I did not meet him in the palace. I met him in a forest hermitage. He is living with his father and mother. His father is a great King named Dumyatsen. The old man was blinded by a strange accident at the time of his son's birth and an enemy took advantage of him and defeated his Kingdom. He is in exile. Satyavan cares for his father and mother."

The sage Narada stood up. "Your daughter has chosen well, Satyavan is the son of the King of Salwa. He is brilliant and accomplished. The young man is unequaled in strength and grace and generosity." At these words Savitri smiled with pleasure. Then, Narada said, "But, she should choose another husband, for it is destined that Satyavan will die in one year."

Savitri trembled then, but standing tall she looked calmly at her father and the sage, and said, "I can think of no one else as my husband. I will marry Satyavan. My mind is made up. You have taught me that time is nothing at all. What is one week, or one year, or one lifetime if you love truly?"

Pleased with her answer, Narada said to the King, "Your daughter's love is stronger than death. Let her marry Satyavan."

King Dumyatsen at first denied his son's marriage to Savitri. He told Asvapati that the life in a hermitage was a lonely and difficult one, that a princess would not be happy living in a forest. But the King simply stated that his daughter would marry no one but Satyavan. And the blind King admitted that indeed his son had said he would marry no one but Savitri.

The wedding was held in the hermitage. Savitri took off her jeweled crown, her golden bracelets and her silken robes. Satyavan and Savitri knew wealth in their love. Everyday they grew to know each other better and they experienced supreme joy. As a wife Savitri was generous and dutiful. She helped care for Satyavan's parents without hesitation. As a husband, Satyavan was devoted and kind. Their days in the forest were happy.

But, underneath her happiness, Savitri was sorrowful. She knew that with each day her husband's life grew shorter. When it was four days before his destined death, Savitri began a fast and she meditated without interruption. Satyavan respected her wishes to give thanks to the Goddess who had brought them such joy, but he looked forward to the end of her four days' austerities.

On the fourth morning, Satyavan said he would go out and gather fruit and chop wood to build a fire now that her fast was nearly ended. As he set off for the forest alone, his wife said, "Let me go with you. I am refreshed by my devotion and would like to walk among the trees." She had never asked for anything before, so the old King and the Queen and their son, who feared she was too weak to travel, granted her wish.

Satyavan walked cheerfully, pointing out all the new blossoms in the forest. Savitri walked beside him silently. She never took her eyes off his face. They gathered fruits, and then stopped to chop wood. She sat on the ground and watched her young and virile husband wield an ax. And the sound of the ax echoed among the trees.

Suddenly, the axe fell from his hands.

"I have a headache," he said.

Fighting back her tears, Savitri whispered, "Put your head on my knees and rest. It will pass." And he lay down and closed his eyes. She gently caressed him as the color slowly faded from his face.

As she comforted him, she felt a presence. Looking up, she saw standing before her a tall figure dressed in red. His hair was tied in a topknot, and in his right hand he held a noose.

"Who are you and what do you want?" she asked.

"Young woman, you must be extraordinarily sensitive to see me. Few see me and fewer less speak to me, although everyone knows who I am. My name is Yama. I am the Lord of Death."

"Why did you come? Don't you usually send your messengers?"

Yama answered, "Your husband's nature is possessed of such goodness that I came myself."

Then the Lord of Death took his noose and extracted the life essence from Satyavan, turned and began walking south. Savitri lifted her husband's head and set his body carefully on the earth. Then she turned and quickly walked after Death.

"Young woman," he said, "the living do not go where I am going. You must prepare a funeral for your husband. Turn around. Follow me no further."

"I go where my husband goes," answered Savitri. "Sir, is it not true that a wife can be faithful to her husband even after he is dead?"

Yama stopped and shook his head, "Yes. Even after death a wife can be faithful. But you cannot enter the land of the dead." He grew thoughtful. "What you say pleases me. I will grant you one boon, but not for the life of your husband, and follow me no further."

"Could you return the eyesight of my father in law?"

"It is done," spoke Death, and he continued walking south. But Savitri followed after him.

"It is cold where I am going. Go no further," he commanded.

"Excuse me for my disobedience, but it is so rare to have the opportunity to speak to someone with your virtues. May I not ask you several questions?"

Yama was pleased. "Ask me your questions."

"Sir, you are the Lord of Death. Does that not mean that you are the Lord of Life as well?"

"Yes. I am the Lord of Life as well. You speak well. So many misunderstand and see me as evil."

She continued, "I have often thought about the true

34

nature of compassion. Most people consider that one should be kind only to one's friends and family. But, does not true compassion mean that one is kind even to one's enemies?"

"If this truth was understood, great happiness would be felt among people. You speak intelligently." He said. "Ask me one more boon, but ask not for the life of your husband and follow me no further."

Savitri requested that her father-in-law's kingdom be returned to him, and Yama agreed. Then, Death turned and walked south once more. Again Savitri followed behind him.

"Young woman, you cannot follow me."

"It is hard to turn and leave when I can partake of the feast of your knowledge." Yama was pleased again and listened to her questions. She asked him about the source of life and the nature of freedom. He said that human beings experience freedom when they understand that human life is precious and impermanent.

They talked for a long time. He answered many of her questions regarding karma and the cycles of cause and effect; about pure thought, right conduct and the nature of devotion. Yama was content with her knowledge and offered her one more boon.

"My father and mother wanted a son but had none. Would you grant me fifteen sons in this lifetime?"

"Certainly," he replied. "You shall have fifteen strong sons. But you have come too far. You must turn back."

This time she followed his instructions and did not move any closer. However, she called after him softly. He stopped again.

"Your voice is beautiful," said Yama. "It is hard to resist you."

"I revere your understanding. But, have I not answered all your questions? Do you desire one more boon?"

"Sir, did you not say that a wife can be faithful to her husband even after death? I ask you to return my husband's life so that I can give birth to fifteen sons."

The Lord of Death gave her back the life of Satyavan. She bowed before him, touching all seven places of her body on the earth in gratitude, knowing that her love and devotion had won back her husband's life.

Swiftly she returned to the body. She held Satyavan's head on her lap. As she caressed him, the color came back to his face.

He awoke startled. It had begun to grow dark.

"I slept so long. I am feeling better. We had best return to my parents quickly or they will think something happened to us. I had a strange dream. I saw Yama standing beside me."

Savitri said, "That dream has come and gone." They walked home through the forest.

In the meantime, the King of Salwa's eyesight miraculously returned. His blindness was cured. And not long after that, messengers came to tell him that his enemies were vanquished and he could return to his kingdom. The days in exile in the hermitage were ended. He took this as an auspicious sign that Savitri and his son were in no danger.

At long last, when the couple returned, Dumyatsen and his venerable wife asked, "What took you so long?"

Savitri answered, "We journeyed much further than we expected." ❧

The Robe of
Love

A merchant decided to make a pilgrimage to Mecca. He dreamed of this journey for many years, but his wife had died leaving him to bring up three daughters. Finally, when the girls were old enough, he was able to make the journey.

He asked each of them, "What shall I bring you from the great marketplace by the Holy City?" The eldest girl requested a necklace of gold. The middle daughter asked for silver bangle bracelets. But, the youngest daughter said, "Father, I seek my heart's desire. Bring me Caftan El Hub, the Robe of Love."

"What does it look like?" inquired the merchant.

"I do not know. An old woman in the market disturbed my peace of mind with a single question. She asked me 'Do you know what you truly want?' I thought about it for many days and then returned to her with my answer. 'I seek my heart's desire,' I said. She said, 'Few seek their heart's desire, and fewer find it. But if that is what you want, you must find Caftan El Hub, the Robe of Love.' Then, the old woman

37

disappeared. That is why I ask for the Robe of Love. But how it looks or how it can be found, I do not know."

The merchant nodded, "In a great city like Mecca, surely I can find the Robe of Love."

In Mecca, the merchant prayed for forty days. He circumambulated the black stone said to have fallen from the sky before recorded time. Then, as he promised, he went to the market to find gifts for his daughters.

He easily found a gold necklace, and the silver bangles, but in no souk could he discover a Robe of Love. He went from merchant to merchant, from stall to stall, finally choosing the finest fabrics in the world for his youngest child. He set off to make the long trip home.

He traveled through the desert.

In the middle of the desert, the merchant stopped in an oasis to rest. The only other traveler was an old man. The man's white beard was so long that the merchant assumed he had great knowledge. He inquired, "Have you ever heard of Caftan El Hub, the Robe of Love?"

The old man responded, "Few seek their heart's desire, and even fewer find it."

"Do you know where I can find such a robe for my youngest daughter?"

The old man explained that the merchant would have to walk north in the desert for twelve days. "You will come to a large tree. Twelve men could not stretch their arms around its trunk. Sit beside it on the sand, what enters your mouth, swallow." He then instructed him to go north another twelve days. "You will come to a river. Sit on the earth. Whatever enters your mouth, swallow. It is not easy to find the Robe of Love."

The merchant changed directions and traveled north. "There are twenty-four hours in a day. Twelve constellations in the sky and twenty-four days in the desert to fulfill my daughter's wish," he thought as he traveled.

After twelve days, he came to the tree. Seated on the sand he opened his mouth and swallowed sand. He traveled again twelve days and this time sat on the ground and swallowed muddy water.

Within moments, a Djinn rose up from the river and called out, "What is it that you seek?"

"I seek the Robe of Love for my youngest daughter," answered the merchant.

"Follow me." The Djinn dove back into the water.

The faithful father walked into the river. To his surprise, he sank, eyes open, mouth breathing. Before him shimmered a white gate of pearls. The Djinn led him through a small door. Inside the merchant saw a palace of gems. It was indescribably beautiful. Inside was a royal court whose walls and floors were made of marble, shell and lapis lazuli. On a gold throne sat the King of Djinns.

Bowing respectfully the merchant asked, "Can you tell me where I can find the Robe of Love for my youngest daughter?" The Djinn King laughed with great delight.

He gave the merchant a piece of sandalwood incense, with the following instructions: "If your daughter is to find the Robe of Love then she must light this incense. When the smoke rises her journey will begin."

The merchant thanked the Djinn King and followed the first Djinn out of the palace. Within moments, he found himself returned to the oasis from where he had begun. The old man was gone and the merchant set off toward home.

The merchant arrived home, weary but heart-refreshed. His three daughters greeted him. When he had rested, bathed and dined, and they had quenched their thirst for conversation, the merchant gave his gifts. The eldest girl was pleased with her necklace and the middle daughter admired her silver bangles. When the youngest sister accepted the piece of sandalwood incense, the others mocked her. "What use is that?" they said. Quickly, she went to her room and lit the incense. As soon as the sweet smelling smoke of sandalwood rose into the air, there was a knock at the door.

A long procession of Djinns stood outside: women and men, children and horses, and a golden carriage. The one Djinn who the merchant recognized, announced, "I have come for your daughter. She will live in a palace, marry a nobleman and shall want for nothing in this world or the other. She will find the Robe of Love."

The merchant worried, "I cannot marry my daughter to a Djinn. She is as close to me as the skin on the palm of my hand, as valuable as the lashes that protect my eyes." But the youngest daughter begged her father, "Let me make the journey."

The two eldest sisters were insulted. "Why should she marry before us?" they demanded. Untouched by their taunts, the youngest climbed into the golden carriage and was taken away as the Djinn assured the merchant that whenever he wanted to see his daughter, he had only to call her name and she would appear again.

The carriage wheels turned on the earth until they were a distance from the merchant's house. Then, it lifted into the air like a winged creature and soared to the edge of a river. The girl hardly noticed the carriage sink beneath the water.

When she did look out, she saw she had descended into another world. The tears that flowed from her eyes overwhelmed the salty taste of the sea. Before her was a tall gate of gems. Then, to her great surprise, the old woman that she had met at the market opened the door into a courtyard before the palace, and invited her to step down from the carriage. The merchant's daughter followed behind the old woman. She found herself in a splendid palace in which was a gorgeous garden that seemed to be hers alone.

"It is my pleasure to fulfill your every need," remarked the old woman kindly. She prepared sweet dishes and lovely drinks and showed her as many fine dresses and adornments as she could ever desire. The kindness of the old woman was the greatest gift. And so the youngest girl forgot her sorrow, athough she never saw the man she was to marry. But after a day or two she thought nothing of it.

She was comforted and lacked for nothing. The old woman taught her everything a girl with no mother should learn. And in the evenings before she went to bed, she was given sweet tea to drink. At night she dreamed of a man. That was sufficient.

One day the two sisters, aggrieved with curiosity, begged their father to call for their youngest sister. No sooner did she appear, carried through the air by spirits unseen, than the sisters began to question her. "Who is your husband?"

"What is it like?"

"Where do you live?"

"Do you enjoy your marriage?"

At first the girl was thrilled to hear the voice of her sisters and comforted by the arms of her father, but the questions were dangerous. The old woman had warned her not to speak too much about the life she led in the palace. She described the palace, and each one of her dresses, to satisfy her sisters. But they persevered, until at last the girl sighed and answered, "There is no husband. I drink some tea before I go to bed and dream each night of a marvelous man. That is all."

"Oh," gasped the sisters in unison, "Don't drink the tea!"

That night she returned to the palace thinking, "How clever my sisters are. I would never have thought twice about the tea." She feigned drinking the tea that night and closed her eyes. She covered herself with silk sheets so the old woman would notice nothing.

At midnight, the bedroom door opened. The man she had dreamed of entered the room. He ate some of the food left on a small table by the old woman, and put on a red silk caftan. He lay down beside the girl, and did not so much as touch her. When his breathing revealed he was asleep, she opened her eyes and stealthily stood up to see him.

She took a candle from the table and lit it. She shone the light on his face. He was handsome, noble, elegant, with black hair like night and red lips like pomegranates. Slowly, she moved the candle downward to stare at his neck, his shoulders, and his chest. In all ways he seemed perfect. Then, she saw that over his heart was a tiny silver door with a tiny silver key dangling on a little hook. She could not resist temptation and took the key in hand and turned the lock to open the little door.

Inside, there was a silver porch and a silver staircase. The girl climbed onto the porch and rushed down the steps. She arrived in a palace in a room adorned with silver thrones and treasures of immense beauty. She opened another door into a room of gold, then another of jewels of every color. She walked through seven rooms dazed by splendor and beauty. Then, at the center of all the rooms was another, an empty room of silence and calm, far more enticing then all the wealth of the world. There she stayed for a moment, until she remembered where she was. For fear she would wake the man, she rushed as quickly as she could, through the rooms, up the stairs, onto the porch and out of the door that covered his heart.

As she was placing the little key back on the tiny hook a drop of hot tallow fell on his skin. He awoke. He smiled, "I should never have let you spend the day with your sisters," he said cheerfully.

"I was only curious," she confessed as he drew her into his arms. He whispered, "Better not be so curious again."

So began their wide-awake love in the night. Every morning when she woke, he was gone leaving the red robe on the edge of the bed. She asked no questions. She was as happy as any young bride was. Time passed happily.

Then one day the sisters, burning with curiosity, had their father call for her again. He did. But the old woman appeared in her place, and warned that if they were not careful, the sister would lose all she had gained. The two sisters feigned kindness and plucked a red rose from their garden and sent it as a gift to their sister in her palace beneath the water.

When the girl smelled the red rose from our world, she longed to go home. She promised the old woman that she would not speak of her husband. The djinn-woman saw that the girl was homesick and had her taken again through the air to her father's house.

This time the sisters' questions were ceaseless. "There must be a man," they demanded. "What is he like?" And finally, before she was about to leave, they pleaded, "At least tell us his name."

She said, "I never asked his name."

"How can you spend the night with a man whose name you do not know?" said the sisters with such certainty that the girl felt ashamed. "We are older than you and know about such things."

That night, certain that her husband would not deny her request, she asked his name. He refused. She asked again. Every night she asked even though he warned her of how much she had to lose.

One night, she said, "If you love me, you will tell me your name."

He asked, "Are you certain you want to know my name?" She answered trembling, "Yes."

He said, "My name is Caftan El Hub. I am the Robe of Love."

His voice echoed like thunder. His body expanded. He filled the room, and the palace, the river, and the world, until he could not be seen. The girl, horrified, fell into a deep faint.

When she opened her eyes, she was lying in the desert. She had lost everything. In every direction she saw nothing but sand. No matter how far she walked she found nothing but sand. It is impossible to say how long she walked. She walked until her feet no longer burned. She wept until she had no tears. She thought only, "I have lost everything, and desire only to be reunited with the beloved."

The merchant's daughter crossed the desert until hope and fear and time did not exist.

One day she saw the walls of a large city. She sold a single bracelet she wore in a market outside the city and purchased the white robes of a religious student. She disguised herself as a young man. She made her way to the mosque in the center of the city and sat outside its walls to pray. There, she began to sing of longing for the beloved. Her voice was filled with such urgent beauty that people gathered around her to listen.

"His words are as sweet as the houris of paradise," they said.

"His throat is alive with the wings of a thousand birds."

News spread quickly that a young religious poet/scholar had arrived in the city whose words of praise equaled the greatest singers of the East. "Even the birds and the insects come to listen," they whispered.

One day the grand vizier, minister to the Sultan, forgot an appointment at court because he stayed too long to listen to the young man's songs. He could not take himself away from what each considered "the sound of the divine." When questioned by the Sultan, the vizier confessed that the prayers of the young man were bliss itself. So the Sultan went to hear him sing.

He too came under the spell of the young man.

"I implore you to sing in my court and my gardens," requested the Sultan.

But the young man answered, "I will not move from this place."

"Your words will inspire me to justice, and the sound of

your voice will refresh heaven and earth," said the Sultan and offered him anything his heart desired.

"I desire nothing in this world," the young man said.

"Is there nothing you dream of?" continued the Sultan.

The young man sighed, "I do dream of a palace of worship unequaled in beauty in this world. It has seven rooms surrounding a single domed chamber. Such an edifice on the earth would inspire all toward the divine."

The Sultan rejoiced, "I employ the finest architect in Moroc."

And so it was that the youngest daughter in the guise of a young man sang in the court of the Sultan in the morning and in his gardens in the evening. But, in the shade of the afternoon, she made her heart's dream visible through the art of the architect. Slowly, beside the palace, grew up the most exquisite house of prayer.

Meanwhile, on the upper story of the Sultan's palace, overlooking the gardens, was the room of the Sultan's daughter. She listened every evening to the songs of the young man and fell in love with him. "Father, it is my wish to marry the young scholar who sings in the garden."

The Sultan had grown to love the young man as well and and agreed to speak to him. The young man said, "I have made my vows to the Beloved. In any other lifetime I would gladly marry your daughter."

The news of the young man's rejection broke the Princess' heart and she became ill. No doctor could cure her.

At last, one doctor, who understood the medicine and poison of love, proclaimed, "She is sick with unrequited love. Either the young man must agree to marry her, or he must give his life in exchange for hers."

Sadly the Sultan approached his beloved poet. The poet replied, "That which I have dreamed of has now become manifest. Let me spend one night in the house of prayer that I have fashioned from my broken heart, and in the morning, I will throw myself into the river and gladly give my life in exchange for your daughter's. I willingly enter Paradise to see her live. Then I can unite with the Beloved."

The Princess could not bear the news. That night, unseen, she followed the young man into the house of prayer. She walked through seven rooms: one of silver, one of gold, each constructed with the shining gems of this world. But she saw nothing but the young man who she loved. Until she entered the central domed chamber. There the quiet cured her aching heart.

At the same moment, both the Princess and the young man saw a red silk robe lying on the ground. The scholar lifted off his white robes, and donned the red robe. The Princess now understood why he/she had not married her. At that same moment, both their eyes fell on a tiny silver staircase leading to a silver porch, behind which was a silver door. The merchant's daughter rushed up the silver steps, climbed onto the silver porch, threw open the door, and disappeared.

By the time the Princess crossed the room, the silver door, the porch and the steps vanished.

She took off her royal robes and put on the white robes of a religious student. The princess spent the rest of her life searching for her heart's desire.

As for the girl, she reentered her bedroom. Her husband, Caftan El Hub, sat waiting for her on their bed. "From the moment I knew your heart's desire, I sought you," he said.

She asked, "Why did I have to make such a difficult journey if we loved one another in the beginning?"

The Robe of Love laughed as he gathered his wife in his arms. "Although your heart recognized me as the mantle of love, you did not trust your knowing. You had to make the journey. You learned to pray until you became the prayer. It is not given for us each to know all things at once. And those who seek our heart's desire must make the journey." ❦

My heart sleeps in the house of hearts. My heart dreams in the house of hearts. It does not rest with me. It does not rest in the palm of my hand.

Give me a mouth. I want to talk. Give me my severed legs and I'll walk. Give me hands and arms and fists and I'll shout and curse. I'll crush the skull of the snake. Throw open the door of heaven.

Give me my heart. Let it pump again life's power in me, infuse my hands and feet with spirit. Give me my heart. Let me rise and walk. I am quickened. No more sleep. No more dream. No more death.

— *Egyptian Book of the Dead*

The Boy and The Beggar

A LEGEND FROM KOREA

A young man was sent by his father to study law in the city of Seoul. Because he was from a poor family, the father told him how to behave and which streets to walk through, in order to make certain that his origins were not noticed. The boy followed his father's rule. He dressed properly, studied diligently, made the right friends, and avoided the streets his father designated were inappropriate. As the weeks passed, however, he became curious about the forbidden streets of the poor. They seemed to be the most interesting. They were separated from the main city by an arched white gateway, a crescent moon of stone.

One afternoon, returning home from school, he stopped to stare through the gate into the ghetto streets and saw a remarkable sight. A well-to-do and highly renowned magician, dressed in fine robes, lay down in the dirt on the road before the feet of a filthy beggar. The magistrate's son was astonished. With a nod of his head the beggar signaled the magician to rise and then pass him and enter the arched gate.

47

The magician noticed the boy and remarked, "You are surprised that a man of my stature would kowtow to a beggar. It is obvious with all of your book learning that you have never learned to see. That man who appears to be of the lowest sort is a holy man."

The magician took three grains of rice from his belt, and blew them into the air where they turned into birds as he walked away.

The boy could not stop thinking about the beggar. The next afternoon after his classes he went through the forbidden gate to search for the man. He stared into the faces of the homeless and destitute, until he found the beggar, shivering in a doorway. He dropped coins into his hands and rushed away embarrassed.

Each afternoon the boy found himself returning to the ghetto streets in search of the beggar. He always gave him a coin, or shared his food with him.

The beggar never said a word. But, from time to time he looked up at the boy. His face showed no malice. His eyes were not bitter. The boy could not stay away from the mendicant.

One night, when it was very cold, the boy warmed himself by a small brazier and worried about the old man. He went out into the streets until he found him huddled on the ground against a building. He reached out for him and led him to his rooms. He prepared a warm bath, gave the beggar clothing and food, and let him sleep on the floor beneath thick blankets. Many nights that winter the beggar slept in the boy's room. He never said a word.

Only once the beggar touched his shoulder and smiled. The boy shyly returned the smile. He felt himself loved by the old man. It was as if it was he who took care of the boy. His heart was filled with a love he felt only for his own family.

In the spring, he continued to bring food or coins to the beggar. But his exams soon consumed him. He went less often through the arched gateway. As summer drew near and he readied himself for vacation, he simply forgot about the beggar and left the city for months.

When the student returned in the autumn, the face of the beggar appeared to him as he unlocked the door of his room. He realized that he had hardly given the beggar a thought during his vacation. He had lived as a child again without a care. Now, he rushed through the arched gate in search of his friend. He could not find him.

As he turned to leave the ghetto streets, he saw two beggars carrying a stretcher with a corpse. The beggar lay dead. The boy berated himself, "If only I had not forgotten. If I had left him money or food, he would not have died." As the beggars carried the body away, the boy sat down on the ground and wept.

The magician passed by and saw the boy. He stood before him and looked into the boy's eyes. The boy said, "It is my fault. My selfishness has been the cause of his death."

The magician answered, "You cannot prevent death. And it is not your fault." Looking into the boy's eyes, the magician continued, "You have learned to see a little, but you have not seen everything."

Once again he took out three grains of rice and blowing them into the air turned them into birds.

Soon the student graduated. He became a magistrate and went to work in the village where he was born. He married and had two children. His own parents died. From time to time he thought of the beggar who he had loved, but his work was demanding and his family responsibilities were many.

Then, once, he went on a journey to another city for business. As he traveled by donkey, his mind distracted with this and that, he did not notice that he had taken a wrong turn. The donkey climbed a steep mountain road. When the donkey stopped before a sheer rock mountain unable to go further, the magistrate recognized his dilemma. He attempted to turn the donkey, but the beast was stubborn and stood still. The man climbed from the donkey's back and tried to turn the animal around in the other direction on foot. Again, the donkey would not budge.

Suddenly the magistrate heard a thunderous sound and watched as the mountain opened revealing a passage through the stone. The donkey simply walked into the pass. The magistrate rushed after the animal and heard the stone mountain close behind him. Again, he climbed onto the donkey and went forward. He looked out over a remarkable mountain range soaring above valleys and streams of fresh water. The air was intoxicating. The magistrate became lightheaded and unconcerned with his journey's goal.

Then he saw a procession of noble ladies and gentlemen on horses in the distance. They were dressed in bright colored brocaded robes holding long poles with banners in seven colors. A man, who must have been a Prince, was waving his arms in his direction.

The magistrate turned to see who traveled behind him. But he realized they were welcoming him.

A Prince of great elegance rode ahead of the others. He greeted the magistrate and invited him to his palace to rest and to dine. "I have been waiting for you," remarked the Prince.

The magistrate was delighted by everything. The atmosphere and beauty of the land and the warmth of the royal entourage replaced all caution with a sense of happiness. Once inside the palace he was taken to a room, bathed, given a change of clothing, and invited to dine with the Prince. They began a conversation like long-lost friends. They spoke about everything of pertinence and value. The magistrate talked about his family, and his village and the Prince spoke about his gardens and his court. As the night lengthened, the two men grew silent.

The Prince stared at the magistrate. Then, the magistrate looked carefully at the Prince. The Prince smiled. The man experienced unconditional joy. He returned the smile and then recognized the eyes of the Prince. They were the eyes of the beggar who he had loved as a boy.

The Prince said, "I am the beggar that you befriended in the city of Seoul. I was reborn in that circumstance to develop compassion. You were the only person who showed me great care, although you knew nothing about me. I vowed then that I would show you the hidden world inside this world."

For seven days and seven nights the magistrate remained in the luminous and gentle world of the Prince. Then on the eighth morning, as he walked in the gardens surrounding the palace, a mist gathered around him.

When the mist lifted, he was back before the mountain, his donkey turned toward the road before him. He climbed on the animal's back and continued on his journey.

When his business was complete, before returning home, the magistrate decided to visit the city of Seoul to walk through the forbidden gate into the ghetto streets where he had first met the beggar. Whom should he meet at the gate, but the magician. The magician had aged, but he was still dressed in majestic robes.

The magician seeing the magistrate said, "I see you have at last learned to truly see a man for who he is."

"Yes," answered the magistrate and he politely bowed to the magician.

Then the magician took three grains of rice and blew them into the air turning them into three birds. But, the magistrate was not impressed.

Returning home he told the story of the world within the mountain to everyone. Most people thought it was a fairy-tale or a made-up story. But those who had the eyes to see knew that his story was real. ♥

Shamelessly
orange like a
parrot's beak,
arousing with a lover's
touch the clustered
lotus buds,
I praise this
great wheel the sun—
rising it is an
earring for
the Lady of the East

—*Vidya*

The Rose of Paradise

A FAIRYTALE FROM THE CAUCASUS

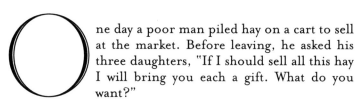ne day a poor man piled hay on a cart to sell at the market. Before leaving, he asked his three daughters, "If I should sell all this hay I will bring you each a gift. What do you want?"

The eldest daughter asked for a mirror in which she could see everything. The second child requested a dress like none other. And the youngest girl asked for the Rose of Paradise. That day the man sold all the hay. Happily, he found the astonishing mirror for his eldest, and a dress like none other for the middle daughter. But, no matter where he looked he could not find a Rose of Paradise.

When he returned home, the youngest daughter stamped her foot and demanded, "Father, I must have the Rose of Paradise." So, the poor man went back to the market to inquire further.

No one in the market had heard of such a flower. On his way home, he asked an old couple walking beside their aging donkey if they had ever seen a Rose of Paradise. They replied, "The Rose of Paradise grows on a tree in the gar-

53

den of a wicked Div. It is impossible to steal it without losing one's life."

The father set off immediately. How he found the garden, I do not know. How far and how long the journey, I also do not know. However, he arrived at the Div's garden. It was surrounded by a tall thick stone wall. The door was wide open and growing on a tree in the middle of the garden was the Rose of Paradise. The Div was asleep at the foot of the tree.

The merchant entered the garden. The Div continued to snore, so he simply reached up and took the Rose without waking him. But, as soon as he was outside the stone wall, the Div awoke and in a violent fury chased after him screaming, "Give me back my Rose of Paradise!"

The father ran as quickly as he could while the Div raced just as quickly behind him. He came to his house and dashed inside, shutting the door. The Div, for reasons that I cannot explain, was not able to enter a house with a closed door. He circled round and round screaming and stomping, "If you do not give me back the Rose of Paradise, then give me your youngest daughter! If not, I will destroy your house."

The youngest girl held the Rose in her hands for a moment, and thanked her father. Then she said, "I wanted the Rose of Paradise to be in this world. Thus, I am the cause of this trouble, and I will go with the Div." She gave the flower back to her father and followed the Div to his world.

From that day forth, the Div called the girl "Rose of Paradise." She became his servant. In addition, she had to serve his sister, the hideous narrow-chested, terrible Divster whose name was Dsudsu Kokoba, The Narrow-Chested One.

One day the Div announced he was bringing relatives for dinner and wanted his sister to kill and cook Rose of Paradise. As soon as the Div departed, Rose, who had overheard the conversation, grabbed a knife from the table and cut the sister into pieces. She piled the demoness into a cooking pot, placed her two narrow breasts on the top, and fixed the lid firmly. Then she built up the fire to cook Dsudsu Kokoba.

Rose of Paradise took a small mirror, a comb, and a

sharp scissors that she saw on a dressing table and escaped. She ran as quickly as she could in the opposite direction from where the Div had brought her. No sooner was she gone, then the Div returned, remarking to his relatives, "Something smells delicious. My sister has prepared a great meal." Not finding anyone at home, he lifted the pot and saw his sister's breasts cooking. He fell into a rage and rushed out in pursuit of Rose of Paradise.

The Div was fast. He nearly caught Rose of Paradise, but the girl threw the mirror behind her. It turned into a glass forest. Confused, the Div raced backward and forward. His arms and legs were cut, but soon he found his way and came upon the girl again. This time she threw the comb behind her. It immediately turned into a forest of thick trees. The Div was slowed as he caught his arms and legs between the branches. But again he found his way and came close to Rose. Weeping and weary she threw the scissors behind her. They turned into blade-sharp scissor-trees, opening and closing. As the Div ran through them his skin tore and bled, but he made his way and soon nearly caught up to Rose again.

She was no match for the Div. She had no more objects to throw and was about to give up hope, when she saw a little house in front of her. She tried the door, but it would not open. So Rose of Paradise fell to her knees and prayed. The door opened. She rushed inside and the door shut behind her.

The Div, who could not open a door into a house, was left outside. He raced 'round and 'round the little house screaming and stomping, tearing up trees and frothing at the mouth. But finally he gave up and returned to his world.

Inside the house it was dark. In the corner was a coffin in which slept a prince. As a boy, the prince had tried to shoot an arrow at the sun, but failed. The sun punished him by making him dead during the day and alive at night. His parents, a King and Queen, placed him in this small house where he lay in a coffin through the day and sat up awake in the dark at night. Each day he was brought food, which he ate, and a candle, which he never lit.

As Rose of Paradise's eyes grew accustomed to the dark she noticed the plate of food and she ate sparingly. At first, she slept each night unseen in a corner of the room. Since the dead-alive prince never lit the candle, he did not notice her. But he soon became aware that every night there was less and less food on his plate. At last he decided to light the candle and look around. He saw a young woman asleep on the floor. She awoke and they each told the other their stories. From that time forward, they spent their nights awake together. And so it was that they fell in love and by the light of a single candle, they became man and wife.

Months passed and Rose of Paradise became pregnant.

"This is no place to give birth," said the Prince.

He instructed her that in her ninth month she should travel north to his parents' palace. "Surrounding the palace are fierce dogs. No one can enter safely. Wear my ring and show it to the dogs. They will lie down quietly and sleep." He told her to go to the Queen and the King and ask for a place to give birth to her child. "I will come to you at night after the child is born. Good luck."

The next morning, Rose of Paradise walked north until she came to the fields that surrounded the palace of the King and Queen. Ferocious dogs began to howl and bark as they rushed toward her. She showed the beasts her ring. The dogs rolled over and fell asleep. In this manner, Rose entered the court of the King and the Queen of that land. They led the strange pregnant girl to a small house that stood beside the palace, within which she could give birth.

That night she gave birth to a baby boy. And the Prince came to the window and called out, "Rose of Paradise, my beloved, do we have a child?"

She answered, "Yes, I have given birth to a son."

"What is the cradle that he sleeps in made from?"

"It is made of old rotten wood."

"And the walls of the room, how do they look?"

"Their color is faded."

"Is there a cover that warms our son?"

"It is a blanket made of rags."

The prince went back to his coffin in the dark little house.

That night a handmaiden to the court overheard the conversation and reported it to the King and his Wife. They asked a different servant to watch again the second night.

Again, the Prince came to the window and the same words were spoken.

When the second servant reported the next day, the King and the Queen called Rose of Paradise to bring her baby to the court. As soon as she walked into the room, the Queen began to weep. "Your baby looks like my son," sobbed the queen. So Rose told her story.

The King and the Queen advised the girl that they would wait in her room that night for their son. But she was not to tell the Prince that they were within.

That night, when the Prince came to the window, he called out, "Rose of Paradise, my beloved, what is the cradle our child sleeps in made of?"

She answered, "It is made of gold."

"And the walls of the room?"

"They are painted the brightest colors."

"Describe the cover that warms our child."

"The cover is woven from soft wool and threaded with silk and gold."

"And are you alone?"

"I am here with only our son."

So, the prince entered the room. The King and the Queen grabbed their son and hoped that in the morning he would remain alive. But, as the sun rose, he fell down dead. At that moment the Queen remembered that her sister was married to the Sun.

"I will go to the house of the Sun and ask for the curse to be lifted," she said.

The Queen set off.

On her way she passed by a house from which arose a terrible wailing cry. She entered to see a pregnant woman sitting on her bed in a wretched state. When the woman heard that the queen was going to the Sun she asked, "I have been pregnant for a year and a half and cannot give birth. Please ask the Sun what I should do." The Queen agreed.

Then, she came to a house where a man was seated inside a burning oven. "Please," he begged when he heard she was going to the Sun. "Ask the Sun how I can get out of this oven."

When she came to the end of the world, the Queen saw a stag with his horns reaching into the clouds. She asked him if she could stand on his back and climb up his horns into the sky.

"Yes, yes," replied the Stag, "If you will only ask the Sun how I can get my horns out of the sky so I can be on my way. I've been stuck for months." She agreed.

When the Queen arrived at the house of the Sun her sister was happy to see her, but warned, "When my husband returns this evening he will want to devour you. Let me hide you and I will speak to my husband on your behalf."

There was a little cottage attached to the house of the Sun. Her sister placed the Queen in a dark room and locked the door with seven iron locks. Then she made a huge meal for her husband. When he returned his wife fed him continuously until he was near to bursting. He asked, "I smell something delicious but I am too full to eat another bite. What is it?" She answered, "It is my sister. She has come to ask you some questions."

As he was falling asleep, the Sun stuttered, "I will gladly answer in the morning."

Before dawn the Sun arose, his belly still full. So he met with the Queen and promised not to devour her. She told him the whole story and asked that the curse on her son be lifted. The Sun agreed. Then he answered the three questions about the pregnant woman, the man in the oven, and the stag with its horns stuck in the sky.

Then the Sun bathed at dawn and gave the water to the Queen to place on her son's head. In this way, the curse would be lifted.

The Queen climbed down the stag's horns and advised him, "The Sun says you should bend your head and move your horns from the clouds and be on your way." So, the stag bent his head and dislodged his horns and was satisfied.

She went to the house of the man in the oven and told the man to step out of the oven, which he did.

Then, she explained to the pregnant woman that she should lie down in the hay and give birth to her child. The woman lay down and pushed the baby out into the world and rejoiced. She thanked the Queen.

When the Queen arrived at the palace she placed the water of dawn on the prince's head and he stayed alive both day and night. The King and the Queen placed two gold thrones in a new court in a new palace beyond the little house beside their own. The Prince sat on one throne. Rose of Paradise sat on the other, and they held their baby in their arms.

As for the old farmer, Rose's father, he was content, as was everyone, because the Rose of Paradise was in the world. And the Prince who was now alive both day and night and the Princess who had made the journey ruled equally and for the benefit of everyone. ❦

You will emerge in springtime

bullrushing in meadows

mud on your heels

shouting

hooray,

it's been a long winter.

—*Steve Clorfeine*

The Tale of Two Souls

ADAPTED FROM A HASSIDIC TALE

The Baal Shem Tov, a great mystic master of Hassidic Judaism, sat at a table to celebrate the wedding of a young couple. He told a story to his guests and disciples. Each listened in his own way. The guests listened with their outer ears alert to the joys of earthly love and the celebration of family and community, while the disciples listened with their inner ears attuned to hear beneath the content, each longing for transcendence.

"Every year for many years, there was a woman who pleaded with me to intercede with God on her behalf. 'Please ask why it is that I and my husband have no child,' she asked. Each year I prayed and received no answer. The woman never gave up her desire. Then, when her back was bent, her hair was white, and she was long past the age of giving birth, I received a message during my prayers. That year, I said to her, 'Go home. God has decided to give you a child.'

"Five years later, she came again. This time she held the hand of a little boy. His black hair was as wild as a mountain goat's windblown coat. His eyes blazed uncannily. 'Master,

I beg you to take this child from me. I am afraid of him. He is not mine.'

"The old woman explained that the boy was a mystery to her, and a burden to her and her husband. 'He is filled with a passion that I cannot comprehend. He seeks as if his young heart was broken. We are simple people. This child is not ordinary.' "

Both guests and disciples wondered why the Great Master had chosen to tell this tale at a wedding. He continued.

He told how he took the boy home and brought him up as his own son. How the child flourished under his care and became a great student of the Torah.

"But everyone could see that the child was yearning for something that no word or prayer could satisfy."

When the boy was sixteen, the Baal Shem Tov described a particular girl to his servants and sent them to a small village in Poland to find her. "If you find this child, ask her parents if they will send her to me so that she can marry my son." Surprised but obedient, the disciples of the Master traveled to that village.

They inquired in every Jewish home. However, no girl of that description was discovered. As they were about to leave the village, they met a poor man struggling beneath a large load of hay on his back. Out of habit, they asked if he had a daughter fitting the description given by their Holy Master.

The old man sighed, "I have six children and the youngest girl fits this description. From the moment of her birth it was as if she was not of this world. She was dreaming of something unknown to us all. The force of her hidden desire frightens my family." He stood silently and then added, "I will gladly send her with you to marry the son of the Holy One, blessed be his name." The disciples rewarded the peasant and took the young woman with them.

As the wedding meal was served, and the Holy One stopped speaking, the disciples discussed the strange tale. Having prayed and studied side by side with so many young men, they were unaware that their teacher had called one of them his son. Others debated over the meaning of this tale that ended so abruptly before the fruition of a marriage. But before the cakes were served, to their further astonishment, the Baal Shem Tov began what appeared to be a new and different story.

"A long time ago in Poland at a time when the Jews were not welcomed in a certain Kingdom, the King had a son who was more interested in learning than in ruling. The King hired a famous scholar, who unbeknownst to him, was a Jew. Every day the teacher instructed the Prince. But, for one hour each day, the scholar requested time alone in a small room, unseen or unheard by anyone.

"The Prince loved his teacher. Yet, the boy knew that there were things of which he did not speak. For when he returned from his hour alone, his eyes were shining and he was filled with an inner joy that the boy found irresistible. Finally, the boy spied on his teacher. He saw him put on the phylacteries and the shawl of a Jew and pray. His teacher's face was glowing. He emanated a peacefulness that aroused the deepest longing in the boy.

" 'It is this experience that I have been seeking,' thought the boy.

"Gaining courage, he told his teacher what he had seen. The man trusted the boy's heart, and revealed that he was a Jew. The boy wanted only to study what his teacher studied. From that day onward, they studied from the Torah in secret together. Reading stories and prayers and psalms, discussing the meaning of words, sounds and images, the boy's heart was enlivened. This is what he had been seeking.

"Soon afterward, in that country, it was declared that all Jews were to be killed. The Prince begged his teacher to take him away with him where they could both safely study. In time, the Jew agreed, and they left in the dark of one night. The King was unable to find his son.

"The Prince was actually a Tzaddik, a holy man. The teacher recognized that such dawning of great wisdom and love was not limited to any religion or country of origin. In a reversal of roles, in the new country, only the boy and the teacher knew that he was not a Jew.

"Several years later, the Prince married the daughter of his teacher. Their love was without demand on each other. They delighted in their mutual kindness and appreciation of prayer. However, at night, as they slept, the girl would awaken to find that her husband's body was still and cold as death. Afraid to disturb him for fear his soul would not find its way back from where it journeyed, she remained petrified until morning. Each dawn, color returned to the young man's face as he awoke. Growing more and more frightened, she begged him to tell her where he traveled.

"The boy confessed that his aspirations and prayers brought him closer and closer to the gates of heaven. 'Please do not be afraid and do not wake me,' he entreated.

"But one evening before falling asleep, he said, 'There is no limit to the love we share. Thus, I make a request.' Then he asked his wife for permission to leave this world. 'Last night I stood before the doors of heaven. I knew that I could enter, but I did not want to leave you without explanation. If you allow me to go now and to unite with God, I will come back in another life and we will be reunited.'

"Reluctantly, she agreed to let her beloved die. That night his body grew cold as his soul soared through the gates of heaven. He did not awake in the morning. It is impossible to describe the depth of sorrow and joy that his wife knew at that moment.

"The young woman herself became a great teacher of the Torah and benefited many people until she too grew old and left this world."

At the end of the second story, the guests and the disciples were silent. Although the story was sad, there was no one who had not felt the intensity of love and longing that the story brought forth from their hearts.

The Baal Shem Tov called for the cakes to be brought to the table. Smiling, he poured the wine. Then, with tears in his eyes, he toasted the young couple saying, "Today this boy, who became my son, and this young woman, who we searched for in a distant village, were that boy and girl from so long ago. They have found each other again. The yearning that consumed them each as children was the unexplainable search for one another, to fulfill a promise made long ago. And, now we celebrate their marriage." 🌰

The Moon Cuckoo

A Tibetan tale retold

A Prince and a minister's son were inseparable friends from childhood. They were as different as day and night. What kept them together was mysterious, but their bond was unbreakable. While the Prince Irini was devoted to the teachings of the Buddha, and spent his evenings in study and meditation, his friend Jalawarla spent his nights studying black magic in the cremation grounds.

In the cremation ground, under the guidance of a magician, Jalawarla developed the power to leave his body and place his spirit in corpses of humans and animals. Once Jalawarla convinced Irini to learn this dark art of the transmigration of the soul. "You will learn far more about your kingdom," urged his friend. In this way they roamed throughout the kingdom unseen.

As time passed, the Prince, seeing the unceasing suffering of all beings, grew more devoted to his Buddhist practice and refused to continue their adventures. He fell in love and married a Princess whose devotion to meditation was as thorough as his own. Therefore, he made Buddhism the spiritual practice of the court. His wife, the Princess Sundrun, was devoted to her husband, and he was faithful to her. Unlike most rulers, he refused all royal concubines.

Meanwhile, Jalawarla grew more confident of his power. A concubine who was rebuffed by the Prince seduced him and slowly convinced him that he should be King and not his friend. Thus, desire and greed replaced friendship.

On a spring morning, Jalawarla suggested to Irini that they spend a day in the outermost gardens of the palace, as they had done when they were boys. The Prince was delighted, hoping to enjoy the love of companionship that had nurtured most of their lives.

They spotted the bedraggled, still-warm bodies of two dead moon cuckoos lying by the side of the river. "Let us place our souls in their bodies and bring them to life," urged Jalawarla. "For the last time. I will never ask it of you again."

To please his friend, and thinking, "What harm can this be?" Irini agreed.

The two young men lay down in the tall grass and abandoned their bodies. They guided their consciousness into the corpses of the birds. There was a strange hush, a sudden breath, and a rustling of wings. The two birds took flight.

They soared, circling, calling out to one another, flying further and further. But Jalawarla, drunk with desire for power, circled far from the Prince and turned alone back again to their starting place. Quickly leaving the body of the bird, he entered into the body of the Prince. He mutilated his own body and threw it into the river. Then he leapt onto the Prince's horse, and leading his own, galloped back to the palace.

When her husband returned in mourning, and she was told of the loss of Jalawarla, Princess Sundrun looked at his face. She shuddered. "I feel that I do not know this man who has returned in sorrow." Fear more piercing than an arrow undid her peace of mind. "He is mourning the loss of his best friend," she convinced herself.

The Prince grieved publicly and fiercely for his friend. He called concubines to his bed and avoided his wife. Princess Sundrun sought refuge in her chambers, thinking, "The death of Jalawarla has changed my husband. How can this be?"

Meanwhile, the moon cuckoo flew back and forth searching for his friend. The Prince feared that Jalawarla was hurt or dead. He found neither the bodies nor the horses and after many days, finally rested on the branch of a tree.

Untrammeled by his human body, the Prince's mind opened restfully. His realization flowered. He sat in silence for hours. Late that night the sky became like day, and he saw endless buddhas, boddhisattvas, devis and devas falling from the sky like snow. Then, when his vision ended, he saw the Buddha sitting cross-legged beneath the tree.

The Buddha spoke. "Your friend has betrayed you. Thus, you have lost two companions."

The Prince asked what had occurred and the Buddha explained, and then said, "As you know, this world is like a dream. Whatever occurs has arisen due to action in the past. Now, I am your sole companion."

The Prince felt unutterable joy and pain. Without his body, the bliss of the presence of the Buddha and the horror of his losses were as keen as a hair in his eye.

The Prince asked, "Does my wife suspect that her husband's soul is not mine?"

"Yes," answered the Buddha. "She knows that."

"Can you tell me what happened in the past?"

"You and Jalawarla were Kings of neighboring palaces. You fought all the time. Thus, your strong unexplainable friendship. In this lifetime, his desire for power overruled his heart, and the consequences could not have been different."

As the Buddha spoke to Irini, the Prince's bitterness and sorrow ceased.

Then the Buddha said, "It is in my power to return you to your body, or to leave you in the body of the bird."

"What will happen to Jalawarla if I return to my body?" asked the Prince.

The Enlightened One nodded his head in such a way that the bird shook with sadness.

"And if I stay in the body of the bird?"

"Jalawarla will continue in his evil way for a long time. Then he will suffer greatly. He will turn to your wife. She will be his teacher in his old age. In the next lifetime, perhaps, he will be enlightened."

"Can you tell my wife what has occurred, so that her suffering is lessened?"

The Buddha agreed, saying that she already understood that the Prince was not her husband. "She knows the illusory nature of this world."

"Then I will stay in the body of the bird," said the Prince.

The Buddha disappeared.

From that day forth, Irini in the body of the cuckoo taught dharma to the birds of this world.

As the years passed, Princess Sundrun's wisdom and compassion increased. Many sought refuge in her presence.

Once a year, she went alone into her private gardens. The sky darkened, and all the birds filled the air with ceaseless song and the fluttering of wings. Then the sound of the moon cuckoo would be heard, the most piercing and lovely cry. She watched as the Prince taught all the birds the path of the way to the cessation of suffering.

When the birds left, the cuckoo remained. For a moment, he lingered on the shoulder of his wife, and she caressed him. Then, together, their spirits soared. ❦

The Boy in the Stone Boat

FROM AN EPIC FAIRYTALE FROM ICELAND

The King and Queen of Iceland had a daughter named Hadvor, who was heir to the throne. They also had another child, a boy they had found as a baby in a stone boat on the beach near their castle. They named him Hermod. He was the same age as their daughter. The boy and the girl became best friends. Even as children they swore that they would marry.

Long before that day arrived, the Queen of Iceland grew ill. When she was dying, she called her husband to her bedside, "I ask only one thing. If you decide to marry again, choose the Queen of Hetland for your wife." The King sadly promised. Soon afterwards his wife died.

One year later, the King set sail for Hetland to seek the Queen's hand in marriage. But a sudden mist covered his boat and he became lost. He found himself near an unfamiliar island and brought his boat to rest on its shore. He walked until he came to a thick forest where he heard the sound of a harp and walked in the direction of the music.

Three women sat in a clearing. One was seated on a gold chair wearing a brocaded dress. The second held a harp in her hands and played a sorrowful song. The third sat silent, wearing a green cloak. She was the servant of the two women.

The woman in the brocaded dress informed the King that she was the Queen of Hetland. She had escaped with her daughter and servant after pirates had plundered her country. Surprised, the King told the story of the mist at sea, the death of his wife, and the promise he had made. He offered to bring the three women to his kingdom. During the voyage to Iceland, he asked the Queen for her hand in marriage and she agreed. Upon reaching his country, he announced his betrothal and a great feast was held in their honor.

The King's two children paid little attention to the new Queen and her daughter. They had their own rooms in their own castle. But, they often played with the servant in the green cloak whose name was Olaf.

One day when the children were nearly grown, the King went to war. No sooner was he gone from the palace than the Queen called for Hermod. "I want you to marry my daughter," she commanded. The young man refused and informed her that he would only marry Hadvor.

The Queen, who was a witch, became enraged and cast a spell on the boy. "You will dwell on a desert island. By day you will live as a lion and by night as a man. You will have only Hadvor to think of, but no Hadvor for your own. The only one who can free you from this plight is Hadvor herself. But first she would have to find you and burn your lion's skin which is impossible."

Hermod said, "If ever this spell should be lifted then you will turn into a rat and your daughter will become a mouse and you will fight each other to the death."

As soon as these words were spoken, the Queen cast her spell and Hermod vanished.

No one in the palace knew what had become of him. The Queen sent soldiers and servants to search for the boy as if she cared, but he could not be found. Hadvor suffered the loss of her friend.

One day the servant Olaf said to the Princess, "I know what has happened to your beloved friend. The Queen is a witch. She has murdered the Queen of Hetland and stolen her face. She has cursed Hermod for loving you and refusing to marry her daughter. She has banished him to an island where he lives as a lion during the day and a man at night, tormented by the thought of you. Only you can free him by burning his lion skin."

Hadvor asked, "Who are you and how do you know this to be true?"

The servant explained that the witch had stolen her away from her home where she had served the queen; but could never do her any harm because of the green cloak she always wore.

"What will become of me?' asked the girl.

"The witch's brother is a three-headed giant who dwells in the Underworld. It is her plan to marry you to him."

The girl said, "There must be something that we can do."

Olaf whispered, "This is what you must do. The giant will come to woo you disguised as a handsome man. He will rise up through the floor of the castle. You must be prepared. When you hear a noise like thunder in the earth, have blazing pitch in a bucket and pour it over the cracks in the floor."

When the King returned from war, he was saddened by the disappearance of Hermod. However, the Queen told him many stories of how ungrateful the boy actually was toward the father who had taken him in when he was found abandoned in a boat. Finally, she convinced the King to forget about the boy.

Day and night Hadvor remained in her castle awaiting the arrival of her demon lover. Nightly she boiled black pitch in a bucket and kept it by her bed. Then one night she heard a rumbling like thunder beneath the floor. The sound grew louder and louder until the floor began to buckle and crack. With the help of the servant she poured pitch on the floor and watched it harden. She heard the demon pushing against the wood, but he could not penetrate her chambers. Then the noise grew less and less until it ceased.

The next morning when the Queen went to the palace gate, she found her brother lying dead in his hideous form. She cast a spell, enchanting him so that the body of the giant was once again the body of a handsome prince.

Then the Queen told the King, "Your daughter is not as she appears. My brother asked for her hand in marriage but she had him murdered. She has an unnatural attachment to the boy that you found by the shore."

In disbelief the King accompanied his wife to the palace gates. When he saw the young man lying dead in the dirt, he said sadly, "He would have been a worthy match for my daughter." Gently, the false Queen added, "Let me think of a punishment to suit the crime."

Then the Queen ordered a burial mound to be built with giant stones. She went back to the King, "I have thought of a suitable punishment," she said, "Let the princess lie in the grave with the corpse of the man she murdered for three days. If her heart is pure, she will survive." Not knowing what else to do, the King agreed.

Olaf, who understood the heinous plans of the witch, warned the girl. "You must find a cloak to cover your clothes when you are laid in the mound. As soon as the mound is closed, the Giant's ghost will walk behind you. Two dogs will accompany him. He will ask you to cut off his legs to feed his dogs, but do not promise to do it unless he tells you what he has done with Hermod. Then he will let you stand on his shoulders as if he was going to let you out of the mound. But he will not. So, when he grabs at your legs, let him hold tight to your cloak, and pull yourself out of the mound leaving the cloak in his hands."

When the mound was finished, the Giant's enchanted body was laid inside and Hadvor was placed alive beside him. The Princess did not resist even when she saw her father's eyes fill with tears.

Once the burial was completed, the ghost of the Giant rose up. The two dogs barked at his feet and he asked the girl to cut off his legs. Hadvor did as the servant had instructed but refused to feed the legs to the dogs unless the giant revealed where Hermod was hidden.

The ghost's voice whistled like a wind rushing through a thin tube, "You will have to take off the soles of my feet and make shoes in order to travel on land and sea to the island where Hermod is kept." Hadvor grabbed for the skin on the bottom of the ghost's feet before the dogs devoured them. Then the giant hoisted her up on his shoulders as if to let her free never suspecting that she knew his plan. As he grabbed for her legs, she let him catch her cloak and as he tried to drag her down, she pulled herself up out of the cloak and out of the earth.

Hadvor ran to the sea. She put the ghost-soul shoes on her feet and walked across the water. She reached the island. There was nothing but sand on the shore and a high row of cliffs beyond. She could see no way to climb the cliffs. Sad and exhausted, she lay down to rest and fell into a deep sleep.

Hadvor dreamed of a tall woman who let a rope down from the cliff to the sand. She set a clew down beside the girl and instructed her to let it lead her to her beloved. She also placed a gold belt on the ground beside where the girl slept, as a protection from hunger.

On waking, Hadvor saw the rope, the clew and the belt. She put on the belt, and climbed easily up the rope. The clew tumbled ahead and led her to the mouth of a cave.

There she hid until evening when she heard the roar of a lion. She watched as the beast shook its skin from its back and turned into the young man she loved. When Hermod lay down, she heard him moan and call out her name in agony. After a long time he fell asleep. Hadvor swiftly took up the lion's skin and burned it. She lay down beside him and rested her head on his shoulder. When he awoke in the morning the spell was broken. They rejoiced to be together again.

However, they had no idea how to find their way off the island. Hadvor told Hermod about her dream. He replied that he knew a witch on the island who he was certain would help them. Quickly they went to the cave where she lived with her fifteen sons. She was the woman in the girl's dream.

The witch said, "Be wary. The giant has turned into a whale that swims in the sea." She lent them a boat and wished them well. Then she told them her secret name, by which she could be called to come to their aid. A name not known to those who set down this story.

That day the two lovers departed. As they sailed, they saw a whale swimming swiftly toward them. The water began to roil and the waves crashed. So Hadvor called out the secret name of the witch. In moments another whale appeared followed by fifteen smaller whales. A fierce battle ensued in the sea. The water rose so high that the young man and the young woman could not see who was the victor or who was destroyed.

Suddenly, the water grew still. It turned blood red. The large whale and the fifteen smaller whales swam back toward the island.

At that moment, in the King's palace, a strange thing occurred. The Queen and her daughter disappeared. A filthy rat and a frantic mouse were seen racing around the kitchen fighting with one another. The servants tried to drive them away, but they were too quick. The King, who assumed his daughter was dead when she never returned from the mound, and who had now lost his wife, paid no attention to the small matter of a rat and a mouse creating havoc in the kitchen. He withdrew to his rooms in sorrow.

One evening, weeks later, Hermod entered the palace alone. He was wearing a sword on his side. After greeting the King, who was startled by his return, Hermod quickly excused himself explaining that he would tell his story that night. He went to the kitchen where the rat and the mouse were still at war. With one swift motion, he slit the rodents in two. The body of the witch and her despicable daughter lay dead on the floor.

Hermod told the story of the witch to the King, who was glad to be rid of the false wife. Then the young man gladdened the King's sad heart with the news that his daughter was alive. He asked for Hadvor's hand in marriage, and of course the King agreed. Havdor returned and everyone rejoiced.

That night, Olaf, the servant wearing the green cloak, told the story of the murder of her mistress, the Queen of Hetland, who had been stolen away in a stone boat by the witch many years before. The Queen had a beautiful baby boy who she hid in the boat. "I stayed with her when she was taken prisoner by the witch so the baby would not be seen," Olaf sadly said. She then told of the sorrowful death of her Queen, the baby's mysterious disappearance and her own long imprisonment.

Then the King told the story of how a baby boy, whom he named Hermod, was found in a stone boat on the shore near his palace.

The young people, who had loved each other since they were children were wed that night. Both their mothers' blessings were fulfilled. And they ruled happily ever after for the benefit of everyone. ❦

When, with breaking heart,

I realize

This world is only a dream,

The oak tree looks radiant.

—*Anryu Suharu*

Krishna and Radha

FROM INDIA

Krishna, "the dark one," appeared in our world as the embodiment of love at the start of the Kali Yuga (the age of strife) in which we now live. He was born as the eighth child of Devaki, the sister of an evil king named Kamsa. The King's astrologers prophesied that a child of Devaki's would kill him. Thus, the King ordered each of his sister's eight children destroyed. The first six were murdered. The seventh escaped, and Krishna, the youngest, was hidden in the household of a cowherd, and escaped death.

In a previous lifetime Krishna, an incarnation of the god Vishnu, was born as King Rama (of the Ramayana) famed for his devotion to his wife Sita. He was so beloved at that time that all the gods desired him. Because he was faithful to Sita in that lifetime, he promised to return as the God of Love in a later era. The Gods vowed to return as cowherdesses and become his lovers.

So it was that in the household of the foster parents of Krishna there were innumerable gopis (cowherdesses) as well. As a baby, Krishna's body emanated a charm and beauty that the cowherdesses could not resist. His mischief was legendary. The evil King Kamsa, however, discovered that his sister's eighth baby was alive, and in a fury he commanded the child-murdering Rakshasa (demoness) named Putana ("stinking") to kill the baby who was secreted in the household of the cowherd and his wife.

In a past life Putana had been Ratnamala, the daughter of a demon King. During a sacrifice, she saw a dwarf (who was an incarnation of Vishnu) and was overcome with motherly love. She longed to have a son as sweet as the dwarf who could awaken such deep love within her demon's heart. Her desire was sincere. So, Vishnu promised that at a later time, she would be reborn as a nursemaid and suckle the reborn God, and attain complete liberation from her state as a demon.

Putana, like the gopis, had no memory of her past life. Under the command of King Kamsa she set out gleefully to kill the baby Krishna. She disguised herself as a beautiful and kind young woman and won over the child's foster mother who hired her immediately as a nursemaid.

When Putana took the baby in her arms she was startled by a flood of confused feelings. Her demon-like rage was accompanied by an overshadowing softness of heart. The child's face, even with closed eyes, was so lovely she could not ignore its effect. Her breasts swelled and her eyes filled with tears. For a moment she forgot her own nature. She throbbed with the pungent love of a mother. Then, she recalled the words of the King, and thrusting the baby back in his cradle, swiftly moved away to strengthen her innermost feelings of vengeance and ill-will. She reached for the baby again and bared her cold breast while lifting him up to suck. Her dry eyes widened with hate and her body shivered as her breasts filled with poison.

The baby opened his mouth and pressed his hungry lips around her nipple. Krishna's teeth bit into her flesh and sucked her breast with divine strength. Putana began to scream. She tried to rip the child from her body. It was impossible. Terrified, the mother of the baby entered the room. The gopis raced to the cradle. And before their eyes, while the infant held fast and sucked poison from her breast, the seemingly lovely young woman transformed into the demon that she was and fell backward, dead. Her hideous body lay on the floor.

The mother took the baby in her arms and placed him in his cradle. The gopis swooned. They were surprised and ashamed to find themselves trembling with sexual desire for the infant.

Later that day the body of the demoness was burned and a sweet smell rose from the pyre. No one could explain the strange event. Only Krishna understood that at the moment of her death, cleansed of poison, Putana, as promised, was liberated through love.

From that night, the gopis dreamed that the infant left his baby body and taking the form of a man ravished them in their beds. However, in the mornings, there was the child Krishna playing his flute and teasing them as he was wont to do in his childish manner. None revealed their odd night dream to the others. The love play of the god was disarming.

One night, when Krishna was grown, holding a lotus like a sceptre, he went into the forest with his flute. He began to play such intoxicating music that the gopis awoke. They threw off their covers, and half-dressed, left their husband's beds to find him. They were at first dismayed to discover his game. Each had thought she was the only one. But the Master of Love enticed them each with his lips and his mouth, his music and his tongue, until each young woman's heart was disheveled and her passion aroused beyond anything they had experienced before.

At the moment when each one was drowned in unabashed desire, aroused to a point of exhilaration, Krishna disappeared. Distraught, they scratched their skin and sought him again, searching the forest in desperation. And, then again, as suddenly, he appeared.

This time he stood in the center of the forest clearing. The gopis, magnetized by his presence, surrounded him, taking hands with one another. The music enchanted them. They lifted their legs, their skirts; revealed their breasts as they danced, circling and laughing. Until, Radha, the daughter of Krishna's foster mother, the one who he desired most, and who had resisted his first song, could not remain aloof. She left her husband's bed and raced like a wild deer into the woods. The sight of Radha caused

Krishna to drop the flute and the lotus he held. She entered the circle in her radiance while he made a bed of flowers on the earth.

Radha ("supreme nature") was his consort, his beloved, the fulfillment of bliss. And, on a bed of flowers on the earth, circled round by gopis and their longing, Radha and Krishna embraced and made love. Their union was exquisite. While they engaged in every pleasure and lustfilled ploy, Krishna became a thousand lovers and satisfied each cowherdess as if she was the only one. All night they moved in the consuming luxury of delight. Even the gods and goddesses, the trees and grass, found it impossible to resist this dance.

Before the sun rose, their lovemaking ceased. Like those gone mad, eyes glazed, lips torn, hearts wild, hair unknotted, bodies sweating, they all ran together to the river. Laughing and singing, they threw themselves into the icy waters and played together until they returned to normal. Then, all the women quietly returned to their homes. ❦

A Riddle: Name me and you destroy me.

The Answer: Silence.

—*Source unknown*

If someone says to you:
"In the fortified city of the imperishable,
our body, there is a lotus
and in this lotus a tiny space:
what does it contain that one
should desire to know it?"

You must reply:
"As vast as this space without
is the tiny space within your heart:
heaven and earth are found in it,
fire and air, sun and moon,
lightening and the constellations,
whatever belongs to you here below
and all that doesn't,
all this is gathered in that tiny space
within your heart."

—*Chandogya Upanishad 8.1.2-3*

Afterword:
Of Bees and
A Bird

One summer, I was telling stories in a tent on a grassy meadow at the foot of a hill in Wales. It had once been a jousting field. Above the tent stood an eleventh century castle. Two bees flew beneath my skirt and stung me on the thigh. Because my audience was absorbed in a tale I was telling, I continued with the story while smarting from an ever-increasing pain.

When the story was over, I pulled out the stingers, applied a salve, and went for a walk to heal my leg. I was drawn to a small tent where a Tibetan man displayed colorful wool rugs and fur hats — a futile business on a hot July day. A knot of eternity emblazoned on a turquoise banner flew above the tent. The salesman was talking to a tall man whose lanky legs stuck out beyond the rugs. I had to stand close to the seated man. He tried to tuck in his legs, which didn't work. He nearly flipped off his seat. We both laughed and suddenly gasped. Our eyes met, like the characters in a fairytale, caught unaware by a feeling of inevitability, or destiny. It was as if an arrow rose up from my heart and shot through my eyes into his.

My heartbeat was so uncontrolled that I became awkward, idiotic and unnerved. My words sounded flat and I stuttered. I felt shy, feeling my cheeks redden. But I found it impossible to walk away, although I wanted to flee. I nearly missed my next performance. I knew the man was also stupefied by the sudden intensity of our connection.

For the next forty-eight hours we walked, talked, drank tea, rested, bathed and recited poetry...in a small room in the castle tower, on stone walls overlooking the sea, and in sculpture-studded gardens surrounding the castle. We fell in love. I was consumed, confused and happy. The unconditional nature of my response overwhelmed me. So, I asked him to leave so I could continue my performances the next day. He left. Immediately I was alarmed by his absence. I didn't know if I would ever see him again. I made phone call upon unabashed phone call. Not finding him home left me trembling. My insides turned into a beehive. My mind was a washing machine of anxiety, regret and desire.

At home in New York, days later, far from the castle, two things happened simultaneously: he phoned me, weeping and reciting Yeats' poetry explaining that he had been away; while, at my window, a starling flew into the glass screeching, beak open, while sparrows and pigeons stood by. I told him about the bird. He said, "That is me." I did not recall that starlings are thieves who often steal the eggs of other birds. Or, that they are not native to Manhattan, but are imports from England. I was too smitten for logic or research. My rapture was more piercing than birds flying into glass or bees flying under my skirt.

For months I flew back and forth between England and New York ruining projects and spending savings. I did not resist the dark call of romance. I never met him in his home. However, six months later he promised to come to my home for two weeks. I waited. He never appeared. Nor did he phone. I called daily. He never answered. I fell into a heartbreak of despair. All my childhood abandonments crowded my consciousness with ferocity and I deemed myself loveless and betrayed. My mind transformed into a hunter for hope. A seeker of clues. A pursuer of possibilities. A dreamer of what might have happened. It felt like hope was torn like a limb lost in a terrible accident. My heart was broken, shattered.

A month later, in Israel, while performing in a festival, I was relegated to a hotel for two days as a result of a terrorist bombing. I cried without relief. The senseless violence exacerbated my senseless loss of love. I flew to England and in an almost supernatural dedication of purpose, I found him. We talked for a few hours. Reluctantly, he told his own tale of despair and confusion. He lived with a woman. He had fallen in love with me, but he could not find the courage to tell me about his other life. "If I had come to New York I would have been destroyed," he said. I could barely tolerate the disappointment that I felt. Sorrow soared through me in waves. I was unable to sleep. I realized, I could no longer repair myself as I had done in the past.

I have no idea why this particular romance was so painful. The only conclusion I can make is that it was karmic. I had magnetized my own needed demise. It seemed unavoidable. That night, in the hotel in England, I gave up the pursuit of love, and made a decision to seek within myself that which I thought I could find outside myself. I vowed that I would not "fall in love" until I had healed, revealed or discovered what part of myself I had abandoned in my painful seeking of wounded and wounding lovers. I would meet Love before I fell in Love again.

I changed. It took years. I literally laid down for hours each day the first year allowing myself to sink deeper and deeper into what appeared to be layers of fathomless suffering. Until, feeling I had touched my basement of disappointment, I returned to my life and vowed to avoid the painful arrows of love. Yet, secretly, I remained wounded and angry. Such extreme behavior could not possibly have resulted from meeting this particular person.

There is a tale about Aphrodite, Goddess of Beauty. She went for a walk with her son Eros, God of Love. She saw Hades rise up from the underworld. His faceless image was barren of joy. His body was hard. She grew angry. Then, suddenly feeling sorry for Him she commanded Eros to shoot his arrows. And, Death was pierced in the heart with Love.

Writing about Krishna I saw the gift of this punishing

love affair. I let the arrow pierce my hidden shadows and recognized my disappointing romance as the teeth of the God of Love sucking poison from my breast. I offered up my anger and attachment to my wound. I dreamed that I was in a marketplace in a meadow. I saw a tall dark-haired man. Relieved to find one another after so long apart, we embraced.

The tales of Krishna's life are often framed in a conversation between a Great Sage and a King. The King, having heard the stories of Krishna, complained, "How can you tell a story that has so little virtue about a married woman who leaves her husband's bed to make love to someone else at night?" The sage answered that even a God's desire is aroused by Love, and that gods cannot be judged in the same way as humans. The King pursued his argument and was finally told by the Sage, "On hearing these stories our conventional limits of love are extended beyond logic and we open into the vastest experience of the Divine within ourselves, which is true love."

So it is with the tales that we read, and the tales of our own lives that we choose to tell. In the visceral imagined reliving within of these tales, our capacity for love is stretched and opens beyond convention or the limits of what we have thought possible. That is the gift of the story. That is the Robe of Love. ♥

Alexander the Great saw two shining eyes in the window of a shop. He was overwhelmed with the desire to own them. "Sell me these eyes," he said. The shopkeeper explained he would sell them for the weight of equal gold against the eyes on a balance. Alexander, a man of adventure, agreed. But the balance holding the eyes did not move no matter how much gold the hero placed on the scale. The shopkeeper said, "These eyes are your eyes that see no end to desire."

—*Herodotus*

Notes

p. xv. Oliver, Mary. "Wild Geese" from *Dream Work* (Grove/Atlantic Inc., 1986)

p. xvi. Helminski, Camille Adams, *Rumi Daylight* (Shambhala Books, 1994) p.17.

p.1-7. The Mistress of Disguise was adapted from a tale found in *Causcasian Folk-Tales* collected by Alfred Dere (J.M. Dent & Sons LTD., 1925) The title in the book is *Helena, The Beautiful*. The only other collection of Caucasian tales I know is by Von Der Leyen, Begrundet von Friedrich, *Marchen aus den Kaukasus* (Eugen Diederichs Verlag , 1989).

p.8. Cassian,Nina, *Life Sentence: Selected Poems* (WW Norton, NY, 1990, p.27). Her poem was sent to me by Steve Sanfield. She is considered the greatest living Romanian poet.

p.9-12. The Garden Woman is my English translation and reconstruction of a tale told by French storyteller Muriel Bloch. She gave me permission to retell it. Her version can be found in *La Femme Jardin Et Autres Contes Extravagants*. Collected and written by Muriel Bloch (Syros Pub., France, 2000) There are similar tales in Greece, Armenia, and the south of France.

p. 13-19. Diarmud's Longing is from a tale entitled "The Daughter of the King of Underwaves," told to me by Mary Platt and retold with her permission. A version can be found by Lady Gregory, *Gods and Fighting Men* (Colin Smythe Gerrards Cross, England, 1904) pp. 253-258. Her version comes from a Scottish variant collected in the 1850s. To read more tales about the Fianna see Heaney, Marie. *Over Nine Waves: A Book of Irish Legends* (Faber and Faber, 1994).

p. 20. Bloch, Ariel and Bloch, Chana. *The Song of Songs* (University of California Press, 1995) p.83. My first encounter with the esoteric meaning came from a midrash class with Amichai Lau Levi in New York City. I am grateful to him for the inner meanings of these lines.

p. 21-22. The Golden Tree. I was mostly influenced by an oral telling by Anita Graham. *Elijah's Violin and Other Jewish Tales* (Harper & Row, 1983) is her source.

p. 23-26. Sandalwood Leaves. One of the Tales of the *Haft Paykar* *(The Seven Pavilions)*. An excellent and readable version can be found in Chelkowski, Peter J., *Mirror of The Invisible World: Tales From The Khamseh of Nizami* (The Metropolitan Museum of Art ,1975). Another version was translated by Julie Scott Meisami, Ganjavi Nizami's *The Haft Paykar: A Medieval Persian Romance*. (Oxford Press, 1995).

p. 27-29. The Magic Drum. This tale is reconstructed from an Inuit story I recall hearing over twenty five years ago told by Gioia Timpanelli. A variant source is *Tales From the Igloo*, edited by Maurice Metayer (St. Martin's Press, NY, 1972). Other sources of Inuit tales can be found in Ostermann, H., ed., *The Alaskan Eskimos, As Described in the Posthumous Notes of Dr. Knud Rasmussen* (Copenhagen: Gyldendalske Boghandel, Nordsk Forlag, 1952). I was also very inspired by Nor Hall, *The Moon And The Virgin* (Harper and Row, 1980).

p. 30. From a poem by Irish poet, Sally Wheeler, "Open and Shut" from *Word of Mouth* (The Blackstaff Press, 1996) p. 68.

p. 31-36. Savitri. Two excellent variants can be found in: The Sister Nivedita & Coomaraswamy, Ananda K., *Myths and Legends: Hindus and Buddhists,* and *The Mahabharata* (David D. Nickerson & Company, 1923) p.118-216. Sa'Vitri means activator; Satya'van means truth-speaker; Na'ra-da, was a great rishi or sage who was a musician and messenger of the gods. He was the one who related the entire Ramayana to Valmiki. The *Mahabharata* (which means Great Story) and the *Ramayana* are the two great epics of India.

p. 37-45. The Robe of Love was inspired by a story collected by Jan Knappert in a booklet published by Outrigger Publishers (New Zealand, 1975) entitled *Tales of Mystery and Miracle from Morocco*. Jan Knappert heard the tale in 1975. I have taken the most liberties with this story. The ending of the tale is my own invention. I have been telling the tale for over twenty-five years.

p. 46. Giving a Heart to Osiris is from *The Egyptian Book of the Dead*, retranslated by Normandi Ellis as *Awakening Osiris* (Grand Rapids: Phanes Press, 1988).

p. 47-51. The Boy and The Beggar is a retelling from a tale by Jewett, Eleanore M., *Which Was Witch* (The Viking Press, 1953) p.47-58.

p. 52. Schelling, Andrew, *Dropping the Bow: Poems from Ancient India* (Broken Moon Press, 1991) p.12.

p. 53-59. The Rose of Paradise. Dirr, Adolf, *Causcasian Folk-Tales* (J.M. Dent & Sons LTD. 1925.) I simply fell in love with the oddity of this story and began to explore it. I was able to uncover an inner level of meaning as an opening of the chakras of the body, from lowest to most upper. The Rose is symbolic of enlightenment, of the heart, and the essence of Divine Presence. A Div is a spirit being. There are good and evil Divs.

p. 60. Clorfeine, Steve, "Men Are Hungry For Secret Meals," *Beginning Again* (Advocate Press, 1994) p. 13.

p. 61-64. The Tale of Two Souls was first told to me by storyteller Heather Forest when she was nine months pregnant. A beautiful version that I leaned on heavily in the reconstruction of the story is from Levin, Meyer, *Classic Hassidic Tales* (The Citadel Press, 1966).

p. 65-68. The Moon Cuckoo, a Tibetan tale, is adapted from Conze, Edward, *The Buddha's Law Among the Birds* (Cassirer, 1974) and Harris, Rosemary, "Irani and the Cuckoos," *The Lotus & the Grail: Legends from East to West,* (Faber & Faber, 1974) p. 11-26.

p. 77-80. Krishna and Radha was inspired by my friend Marlene Pitkow's article "Putana's Salvation in Kathakali: Embodying the Sacred Journey."(*Asian Theatre Journal*, vol. 18 no. 2 , Fall 2001), pp.238-248. I used many variants and books in order to construct my version: O'Flaherty, Wendy, *Hindu Myths* (Penguin Books, 1975), Campbell, Joseph, *The Mask of God: Oriental Mythology* (The Viking Press, 1962), Dimmitt, Cornelia & Van Buitenen J. A. B., *Classical*

Hindu Mythology (Temple University Press 1978), Hawley, John Stratton and Wulff, Donna Marie, *Devi Goddesses of India* (University of California Press, 1996), and Danielou, Alain, *The Gods of India* (Inner Traditions, 1985).

p.82. This translation is found in the gorgeous book of photos by Michaud, Roland and Sabrina, *Mirror of India* (Thames and Hudson, 1990).

And if Love comes along, it can find in you the unlimited space, the place without end that is necessary and favorable to it. Only when you are lost can love find itself in you without losing its way.

—*Helene Cixous*

NEW PALTZ ᖍᖌ NEW YORK

About Codhill Press

There is no more important function of a writer in our time than to call us to awaken. The state of siege under which human consciousness — human conscience — lives has not abated since Blake wrote, "Truth can never be told so as to be understood and not be believed." Codhill Press is devoted exclusively to the advancement and appreciation of the finest works in poetry and prose which promise to search out important meanings for our lives.

To join Codhill Press' mailing list or find out about other Codhill titles, please write to:

Codhill Press
One Arden Lane
New Paltz, NY 12561

email us at: **mailinglist@codhill.com** *or visit us online at* **www.codhill.com**